GUINEA PIG IN THE GARAGE

Mandy and James looked through the window of the small cubicle that served as an office.

James was about to knock on the door, but Mr. Farmer looked up and saw them first.

"Hello, James, Mandy. What can I do for you?"

"We've brought the guinea pigs down from Johnny Foster's house," said Mandy.

Mr. Farmer frowned. "Well, I'm sorry you've both gone to so much trouble," he said. "But I'm afraid you're going to have to turn right around and take them back again. Rachel knows very well she's not allowed to have pets!"

Mandy and James looked at each other. What on earth were they going to do now?

Give someone you love a home!
Read about the animals of Animal Ark™

GUINEA PIG in the GARAGE

Ben M. Baglio

Illustrations by Shelagh McNicholas

Cover illustration by
Mary Ann Lasher

AN
APPLE
PAPERBACK

SCHOLASTIC INC.
New York Toronto London Auckland Sydney
Mexico City New Delhi Hong Kong

No part of this publication may be reproduced in whole or in part, or stored in a retrieval system, or transmitted in any form or by any means, electronic, mechanical, photocopying, recording, or otherwise, without written permission of the publisher. For information regarding permission, write to Working Partners Limited, 1 Albion Place, London W6 0QT, United Kingdom.

ISBN 0-439-23018-7

Text copyright © 1996 by Working Partners Limited.
Original series created by Ben M. Baglio.
Illustrations copyright © 1996 by Shelagh McNicholas.

All rights reserved. Published by Scholastic Inc., 555 Broadway, New York, NY 10012, by arrangement with Working Partners Limited. ANIMAL ARK is a trademark of Working Partners Limited. SCHOLASTIC, APPLE PAPERBACKS, and associated logos are trademarks and/or registered trademarks of Scholastic Inc.

12 11   4 5/0

Printed in the U.S.A.   40
First Scholastic printing, January 2001

Special thanks to Linda Kempton.
Thanks also to C. J. Hall,
B.Vet.Med., M.R.C.V.S., for reviewing
the veterinary information contained in this book.

TM

One

Mandy Hope and James Hunter jumped off the school bus as it stopped in Welford, the village where they both lived. They normally biked to school, but very recently the roads had been too icy.

Mandy lifted her face to a flurry of snowflakes. "The first snow of winter," she said happily. "I hope it sticks!"

"I think it might," said James. "These flakes are as big as quarters, and they're not much good for my glasses." He wiped his glasses absentmindedly on his pants as he and Mandy walked through the village together. He was a year younger than Mandy and was her best friend.

"I'll give you a call tomorrow," said Mandy when they

reached the post office. "I'm going to pray for snow, so we can go sledding."

"It's Friday tomorrow," said practical James. "It'll be too dark to go after school."

"Well, Saturday then," said Mandy. "Tomorrow we'll just have to content ourselves with snowballs at lunchtime."

"You hope!" said James, grinning as he waved goodbye.

"Hang on!" Mandy called. "What about the meeting in the village hall tonight?"

"Good thing you reminded me," said James. "I almost forgot."

"Good thing I reminded myself!" said Mandy. "See you later."

Mandy thought with pleasure of the coming meeting. Some of the villagers were getting together to raise money for the animal sanctuary. It was always short of funds, and Betty Hilder, who ran it, struggled to make ends meet.

Mandy made her way home to Animal Ark where she lived with her parents. They were vets and Animal Ark was both home and a veterinary practice. Mandy loved living there. Animals were the most important things in her life, and when she was older she wanted to be a vet, too, like her mom and dad.

Emily and Adam Hope had adopted Mandy after her parents had been killed in a car accident. Mandy had been too young to remember them; now she couldn't imagine being with anyone except the Hopes.

At Animal Ark the waiting room was full. Mandy spotted nine-year-old Johnny Foster, who lived near James. Strange that he didn't have his guinea pigs with him. She smiled and gave him a friendly wave.

"I think that young man's waiting for you," said Jean Knox, the receptionist. "Said he needed to talk to you."

Mandy was just about to go over to Johnny when she turned back to look at Jean more closely. There was something not quite right about her.

"Jean, did you leave home in a hurry this morning?" Mandy was trying hard not to laugh, but she felt an enormous grin spreading across her face.

"Yes, I did, as a matter of fact. The alarm didn't go off, and I'm sure I remembered to set it. Why, what's the matter?" Jean was beginning to look faintly alarmed herself.

Mandy looked at Jean's carefully applied green eyeshadow. She was wearing it on one eye only; the other eye was bare!

"You'd better go and look in the mirror. I'll take over reception for a minute." Mandy's shoulders were shaking with laughter. Poor Jean! She was a great receptionist and everyone loved her, but she was always forgetting things!

Mandy looked contentedly around the waiting room at the collection of animals: dogs, cats, rabbits, and even a lizard! She couldn't think of anything better than being surrounded by animals. Her eyes fell on Johnny Foster again and she called him over.

"Jean said you wanted to talk to me."

Johnny's face clouded over, and Mandy could see that he didn't know how to begin. "Why don't you come and have a glass of milk, and I'll see if I can find us something to eat. Jean'll be back in a minute."

"She's back now," said a voice behind Mandy's shoulder. It was Jean herself — with no eyeshadow and a very red face. "I thought people were giving me funny looks," she said. "Why didn't somebody tell me?"

"I don't think anybody noticed," said Mandy. She put her arm around Jean's shoulder and gave her a hug. "You know me — I don't miss a thing."

Jean smiled. "Go and get yourself a drink. I guess you've got some homework to do."

Johnny followed Mandy into the kitchen where they found a tray of newly baked muffins.

"I bet Grandma made these," said Mandy. "Mom doesn't have a lot of time for baking."

When they were both settled comfortably at the table

with milk and muffins, Johnny got up his courage and plunged straight in.

"It's my guinea pigs," he said. "We're going to my grandma's for the weekend, and I need someone to look after them." He blushed as he said it and busied himself picking crumbs off the plate. "Whoever looks after them would need to take them to her house; Dad doesn't want to leave the shed unlocked while we're away."

"Tomorrow? How come you waited so long?"

Johnny's face got even redder. "I didn't. One of my friends was going to take them but he can't now."

Mandy thought hard. Johnny was a popular kid. He always seemed to be with a group of friends. Surely one of them could help.

"None of my other friends are allowed," he said, as if reading Mandy's thoughts. "Or they've got too many pets already. I thought you might be able to help."

Mandy drank the last of her milk. "I'm sorry, Johnny. We don't have boarding facilities here."

"I know you don't, but I thought *you* could look after them. In the house, not the clinic," he added.

Mandy bit her lip. "Mom and Dad are pretty strict about me having extra animals. I really have as much as I can handle with school and helping out at Animal Ark."

Mandy looked at the little boy's downcast face. It was

awful to be worried about your pets when you loved them as much as Johnny did. She wished she could help.

"I'll tell you what, Johnny. I'll ask as many people as I can think of before tomorrow afternoon. I'll do my very best, I promise."

"The big one's had babies and there's nobody to look after her. She's used to having me around. And the other guinea pig died last week." It all came out in a rush, and Johnny turned red as he tried to fight back the tears that trickled down his face.

Mandy passed him some tissues, and he wiped his face roughly, as if he were angry with himself for crying. When he was calm again, he pulled something from his pocket and dumped it on the table. It was a key and a crumpled piece of paper.

"That's the key to the shed so that you can get to her, but Dad said I was only to use it if absolutely nobody can take the guinea pigs back to their own house. So please, please try to get somebody, Mandy. And this is my grandma's telephone number. Will you call me and let me know what's happening?"

Mandy promised that she would.

"And if you can't find anybody to look after her, you'll still be able to go in and feed her because you've got the key. Here's the instructions." Johnny handed her another piece of paper. "But she'll get lonely without company, so it will be best if you can find somebody to take her and the babies home."

Mandy had the feeling that she'd landed the job of chief feeder without being asked! But she knew she'd enjoy the job, even if she couldn't find anybody to take the animals for the weekend. She couldn't let the poor things starve!

"I promise I'll do my best, Johnny."

"Her name's Brandy, by the way. She knows her name if you call her. And I'm a bit worried about the smallest baby because it doesn't move around like the others."

"Don't worry, Johnny. I'll do what I can," said Mandy.

The little boy looked a lot happier when she finally waved good-bye.

As Mandy was getting ready to go to the village hall that evening, she found a surprise waiting for her.

"Better dress warmly and put on your boots," said Mom, with a smile. "Have you looked outside recently?"

Mandy pulled open the back door excitedly. The yard looked as though it had been sprinkled with sugar. And the snow was coming down in thick, round flakes.

"*Yes!*" shouted Mandy. "Yes!" Her face glowed with excitement, and Dr. Emily laughed at the sight of her.

"I prayed it would stick," said Mandy.

"Well, your prayers have been answered then," said

Dr. Adam, coming into the kitchen. "Do you think you could pray that we don't get called out to some isolated farm in the hills?"

Mandy gave her dad a hug. She knew that having to drive the Land Rover through snowdrifts and then perhaps spend hours with a sick animal in a freezing barn was no one's idea of fun.

"I still like the snow, Dad. I don't ever want to grow up and grumble about it."

Dr. Adam ruffled his daughter's hair. "Of course you don't. You enjoy it while you can."

And Mandy could! She kicked her boots through the soft powder and watched the glorious snowflakes swirling through the light of her flashlight beam. She met several people on their way to the village hall, all bundled up well and carrying flashlights. There weren't any streetlights on the roads.

"Hello, young lady. Nice weather for penguins!"

"Hello, Mr. Pickard. Isn't it great?"

"Great?" said another voice. "Let's just hope we're not snowed in. Like that time a few years back. That was a harsh winter, that was. Couldn't move beyond your own front door."

Mandy smiled. Ernie Bell always spoke of the distant past as if it were yesterday. Perhaps it only seemed like yesterday to him; he was very old.

"Hello, Ernie. You'll have to come sledding with me and James."

"Hmm. We'll see about that."

There was a sort of holiday atmosphere when they got to the village hall. People were shaking out snowy coats and hats, shivering and laughing, exclaiming and talking.

"Hi, Mandy!" It was James, standing at the other side of the hall. He was talking to Rachel and Amy Farmer. Rachel was a year behind James in school and Amy was a couple of years younger.

"I've printed up this poster to advertise Save Our Sanctuary," said James when Mandy joined the little group, "but I can hardly read it now. It's gotten absolutely sopping wet in the snow." James smoothed out the piece of wet paper, a worried frown on his face. Save Our Sanctuary was the name James had come up with for the campaign to raise money for the sanctuary.

"It won't be difficult to run off another copy with that great, new printer of yours," said Mandy.

"Have I told you about it?" asked James, his voice rising with excitement. "It can print in color and . . ."

"Only about twenty-five times," interrupted Mandy, laughing. Although Mandy didn't share James's passion for computers, she forgave him because he loved animals almost as much as she did. Thinking of animals reminded her of poor Johnny and his guinea pigs.

"Johnny Foster was at Animal Ark this evening. He needs somebody to . . ."

Mandy was interrupted by the clapping of hands and a voice saying, "Thank you all for turning out on such a dreadful night, but can we get started now? We've got a lot to get through."

Mrs. Ponsonby was in charge of the Save Our Sanctuary group. Mandy sometimes believed that Mrs. Ponsonby thought she was in charge of the whole village! She beamed importantly from the stage, her blue-rinsed hair still covered by a bright purple beret.

"As I was saying, about Johnny Foster . . ."

"If you could all be seated then, I'll explain exactly what the 'service auction' will involve." Mrs. Ponsonby held on to her purple beret as though a gust of wind might sweep through the village hall at any moment.

"Remind me to tell you about guinea pigs," Mandy said to the others. "Don't forget. It's important."

"Guinea pigs?" Rachel's eyes lit up and her face glowed. "I love guinea pigs."

"I don't," said Amy.

"I know you don't," Rachel said. "I don't know why you're taking part in Save Our Sanctuary at all. You don't even like animals."

"I think Mrs. Ponsonby wants to start," James said tactfully.

Mandy and James both knew that Rachel loved animals and suffered greatly because she wasn't allowed to have a pet. Amy had been bitten by a dog when she was small, and ever since she'd refused to have anything to do with animals.

"Now then, everybody. If we can start, please..." Mrs. Ponsonby clapped her hands as if they were all schoolchildren — adults and all!

"She should have been a hall monitor," whispered James. "All that clapping and that loud voice."

The noise in the hall quieted to a hum as people prepared to listen to Mrs. Ponsonby.

"A 'service auction' is a way of raising money that depends for its success on your time and your talents. Yes, your talents," said Mrs. Ponsonby.

"I don't have any," whispered James. Mandy nudged him to be quiet.

"There will be a real auction, as you know, next Tuesday at the Fox and Goose. Julian Hardy has kindly offered to act as auctioneer. Now, that doesn't give us a lot of time, so we need to put on our thinking caps."

"Oh, no," whispered James, pretending to search his pockets. "I've left mine at home!"

Mandy giggled. "Shh." She nudged him again.

"You will need to think about what services you can offer that other people might be willing to pay for," Mrs. Ponsonby was saying. "For instance, someone has kindly offered to take on a family's ironing for the week. So whoever makes the highest bid at the auction will have their ironing done for them. The service you offer can be as simple as that."

"I wonder what I can do," Mandy said thoughtfully. She admired Betty Hilder's work at the animal sanctuary and wanted to help out if she could.

The rest of the evening was spent discussing the different ways to make money for the sanctuary. Mandy and James were both delighted that such a serious effort was being made to help Betty Hilder.

As Mandy and James were getting ready to go home, Rachel came over to them. "Guinea pigs," she said. "You told us to remind you about guinea pigs."

Mandy clapped her hand to her mouth. "Good thinking, Rachel. I almost forgot." She told them about Johnny Foster and how his guinea pigs needed a home for the weekend.

"No can do, Mandy," said James. "I've got one large Labrador who's almost as bouncy as a kangaroo, a cat, *and* a new computer printer to figure out. My mom and dad'll kill me if I bring anything else home."

But Rachel's face was glowing with excitement. "I'll look after them," she said. "I'd love to look after them!"

Mandy looked around to see where Amy was. She was sitting in a corner of the hall, pulling her boots on. She hadn't heard any of the conversation.

Rachel followed Mandy's gaze. "Oh, you don't need to worry about Amy," she said. "I've got a place where I can keep them so she wouldn't even see them."

"Where?" asked Mandy, feeling somewhat suspicious of this sudden revelation. Was it her imagination or was Rachel frantically trying to think of an answer?

"My dad's garage," said Rachel suddenly. "Amy never goes there, but I'm always helping my dad. I'm going to be a mechanic when I grow up. If I'm not a vet," she added.

Mandy knew this was true; Rachel was always helping her dad in the garage.

"If you're sure," said Mandy, still a little doubtful.

"Positive," said Rachel. "My dad's already suggested that maybe I can keep a pet in the garage. This will be good practice."

"That's great," said James. "Good going, Rachel."

Mandy breathed a sigh of relief. It did sound as though it was okay. It had been a lot easier to solve Johnny Foster's problem than she had thought.

Two

The next morning when Mandy looked out of her bedroom window, the world was completely white. Her heart leaped at the sight. A blanket of snow covered yards, hedges, roads, and hills. What a weekend they were going to have!

By the time Mandy had pulled on her clothes and run downstairs for breakfast, it had started to snow again. Mom was stirring something in a pot. "Oatmeal this morning," she said. "It's definitely oatmeal weather!"

Mandy agreed as she sat down at the big pine table with a bowl of steaming, milky oatmeal in front of her.

"Mandy, I've got some very bad news for you." Dad's face was very serious.

"Adam, stop teasing her," said Dr. Emily.

"Sorry, sweetheart," said Dr. Adam, patting her on the shoulder.

"What's the bad news?" Mandy asked, feeling a mixture of relief and frustration.

"You're not going to be able to go to school today," Dad said. "The snowplows have been out and they've sanded the roads, but more snow is expected. I think you should stay at home."

Mandy's eyes shone with delight. "We'll be able to go sledding, build a snowman, have a snowball fight! No school! Yes!"

"We thought you'd be disappointed," said Dad, grinning. "We don't think there'd be too much trouble getting to school, but if the snow keeps up you might get stranded there."

"What a horrible thought!" said Mandy.

She finished the last spoonful of oatmeal and pushed back her chair. "I've got to call James. We've got loads to do."

The first thing was to get Johnny's guinea pigs over to Rachel's house — after she had done her chores at Animal Ark, of course.

There was only one person in the waiting room when she walked through.

"Lots of weather out there," Jean called cheerfully.

"Not a lot of patients, though," Mandy replied.

"No, well, in this weather people don't come out unless they absolutely have to. Nonemergencies have to wait. I've already had four cancellations." She peered at the appointment book as if she were looking for them.

But when Mandy went in to see Simon, Animal Ark's nurse, she found something there that couldn't wait.

A little cocker spaniel sat on the treatment table. Simon was holding a test tube against a card with different colored stripes on it. The dog's owner, a young woman with long black hair, looked on anxiously.

Mandy looked at Simon inquiringly.

"This little guy's got diabetes," he explained.

"That means the blood sugar level goes up and down, doesn't it?" Mandy asked.

Simon nodded. "So we have to test his levels regularly."

Mandy reached out and stroked the dog's silky ears. He was a beautiful golden color and his coat was like silk.

"He's gorgeous," said Mandy. "What's his name?"

"Timmy," said his owner, stroking the dog's back with long, smooth strokes.

"Does that mean you have to come to the clinic every day?" Mandy asked the dog's owner.

"No," Simon interrupted. "I'm teaching her how to test Timmy's blood sugar levels and also how to give him his insulin injections."

"I'm a little nervous," the young woman confessed.

"I'm not surprised," said Mandy. "Anybody would be, I would think."

"Nothing to it," said Simon. "You'll be amazed at how easy it is once you get the hang of it."

The young woman smiled nervously. "Simon's shown me what to do, and now it's my turn," she said.

Mandy held Timmy close while his owner prepared the injection. She watched as the young woman gently pulled out the skin from the back of Timmy's neck and inserted the needle. The dog didn't even flinch.

"There, I told you there was nothing to it," said Simon.

"I think you had a worse time of it than Timmy," said Mandy. The young woman nodded and smiled. She seemed relieved that the ordeal was over.

"The first time's always the worst," said Simon.

"Did you hear that, Timmy?" asked Mandy, giving the dog a final pat. "It gets better every day!"

On the porch, Mandy pulled on her boots and wrapped herself up in a scarf, hat, coat, and gloves. It looked like a blizzard outside.

Mandy's rabbits got a quick cuddle and some food and were put back into their cozy hutch again. They had some crisp green cabbage leaves to munch on, which they loved.

Back in the house, Mandy had the phone in her hand when it occurred to her that James might have gone to school. She looked at the wild snow outside and hoped that he hadn't.

She was relieved when James himself answered the phone.

"Great, isn't it?" he said, when he heard Mandy's voice. "Are you going sledding?"

"Of course I am!" said Mandy. "But first we need to get Johnny Foster's guinea pigs to Rachel's house. Do you think she went to school?"

"She hasn't," said James. "Her mom called my mom to see if I was going. But Mandy, have you thought how difficult it's going to be to carry guinea pigs around in this weather?"

"Yes, and it's not difficult at all, James. It's easy as pie. We have a perfect transport."

"We do?" James sounded puzzled.

"Our sleds."

"Ah," said James.

"I'll be right over," Mandy promised.

"Mandy!" Dr. Emily came rushing into the kitchen,

twisting her thick red hair back into a knot. "Look in on Grandma and Grandpa, will you? I've given them a call and they seem perfectly okay, but they're not going to be able to get out in this weather. See if there's anything they need, would you? Thank you!" She dashed back into the clinic, her beautiful hair looking tidy once more.

"Okay." Mandy smiled at her mother's retreating figure.

It took Mandy longer than she'd imagined to get to James's house. Pulling a sled and wading through snow that came halfway up your boots took quite some time! And the snow, which was still falling heavily, kept blowing in her eyes.

She managed to drag James away from his new computer printer and down into the shed to get his sled. It hung neatly from two thick nails in the shed wall. Together they lifted it down. Within two minutes, they were off to Johnny Foster's house.

When they got there, they found that there were two sheds in the yard as well as a double garage. They weren't sure which one the guinea pigs were in.

"He did say the shed, not the garage," said Mandy. She took the key from her pocket and slid it into the padlock. It went in all right, but it wouldn't turn. "Not this one," she said.

Neither was it the next one. The key slid in, just as it had the first time, but it wouldn't turn.

"Perhaps it *is* the garage," suggested James.

But it wasn't. When they went to look, they found that the garage door didn't have a keyhole but was opened electronically.

James was frowning. "I wonder if the padlock is frozen. That sometimes happens with my dad's car lock."

"Oh, no!" cried Mandy. "How on earth are we going to get the poor things out then?"

"Dad's got a special spray he uses. I could go and get it."

"Great," said Mandy. "While you're gone, I'll look through the shed windows to see if I can see a cage or anything."

Mandy brushed the snow away and peered through the window of the first shed they'd tried. It was kind of difficult to see anything because the window was so dirty inside and there was a gray cobweb strung across it. She managed to identify an old lawn mower, some plastic flowerpots, and in the far corner, something that looked as though it could be a cage. *Good!* she thought. It looked as though Brandy and her babies were in there.

Before long, James came panting back up the driveway, his face bright red from the cold. "Got it!" he called.

"Good. I think they're in here," Mandy called.

James sprayed the padlock, and Mandy tried the key again. This time it turned beautifully.

"What a relief!" she said. "I had visions of Dad having to knock the door down or something."

The shed felt warm and smelled pleasantly of wood.

"Yes, here they are!" said Mandy, who had gone in first.

"They seem quite cozy in here," said James. "It's a shame to take them out into the snow."

"Yes, it is," said Mandy, crouching down to peer into the wire cage. "But Johnny's left a pile of old blankets here, and we can use them to cover the cage. And he says Brandy's used to company. She doesn't like being left alone."

Mandy opened the door of the cage. Immediately a beautiful brown-and-white guinea pig nosed inquiringly toward her.

"Hello, Brandy. Hello, girl." Mandy lifted the creature gently out of the cage and held her close. She stroked her and knew that the guinea pig was calm and happy to be handled.

"Look at her coat," she said. "It's so glossy. Johnny must look after her really well."

"And the cage is spotless, too," said James. "Mandy, look," he said suddenly. "Look at the babies."

Mandy looked. Scurrying around the cage were three inquisitive and lively babies. They were miniature copies of their mother, with the same glossy brown-and-white coats. She noticed a fourth sitting timidly in a corner. This must be the one that Johnny had mentioned; the one he was worried about. Mandy could see why. He certainly seemed very quiet.

"They're gorgeous," said Mandy. "Aren't they absolutely gorgeous, James?"

James nodded. He was busy trying to close the cage door to stop the nosy ones from escaping.

"Johnny's a bit worried about the quiet one," said Mandy. "Apparently he's always like that."

"Perhaps he's just shy," said James. "There's nothing wrong with that."

Mandy smiled. James was often fairly shy himself.

"We'd better get going," said James. "Off to the Hotel Farmer!" he told the guinea pigs.

The cage fit easily onto James's sled. Mandy covered it with blankets, and side by side they pulled their sleds down into the village. Mandy's sled held the guinea pigs' food.

The snow had not stopped, and Mandy and James were soon covered.

"You look like a snowman," said Mandy. "And you look as if you're pulling a homemade igloo on your sled."

James laughed. The hutch did look a little like an igloo, with its wrapping of snow-covered blankets.

"We'll go sledding after lunch, okay?" he suggested. "I want to take Blackie because he's absolutely nuts about snow. He dashes around like a lunatic, yapping and barking."

Mandy laughed. Blackie was James's black Labrador, absolutely adorable but not the best-trained dog in the world! It would be fun to take him sledding. Knowing Blackie he'd probably sit on the sled with James and enjoy the rides, too!

"I haven't called Rachel to tell her we're coming," said Mandy. "Have you?"

"No," said James.

"I suppose we'd better go straight to the garage," said Mandy. "There's no reason why Amy should even see the guinea pigs."

The Farmers' house was next door to the garage but set some distance away from it, halfway down a very long yard.

Rachel's father was an excellent car mechanic and owned the garage himself. It was a big place with an inspection pit and ramps and all sorts of machinery.

When Mandy and James arrived, there was no sign of Rachel or Mr. Farmer. But a couple of mechanics were working inside.

"Have you seen Rachel?" Mandy asked one of them.

The man stood up and wiped his hands on his overalls. "She was in here earlier, helping me with some new tires." The man smiled. "But I think she's gone back home now. Mr. Farmer's in the office if you want him."

Mandy and James looked through the window of the small cubicle that served as an office.

James was about to knock on the door, but Mr. Farmer looked up and saw them first.

"Hello, James, Mandy. What can I do for you?"

"We've brought the guinea pigs down from Johnny Foster's house," said Mandy.

Mr. Farmer frowned. "Well, I'm very sorry you've both gone to so much trouble," he said. "But I'm afraid you're going to have to turn right around and take them back again. I've had a talk with Rachel this morning. She knows very well she's not allowed to have pets!"

Mandy and James looked at each other. What on earth were they going to do now?

Three

Mandy knocked determinedly at the Farmers' back door. She and James had left Brandy and her babies behind a bush near the front gate. It was the perfect sheltered place, and the guinea pigs were still covered with warm blankets.

It was Rachel herself who opened the door. Mandy could see that she'd been crying, and the sight of the young girl's tear-streaked face stopped Mandy from giving her a piece of her mind.

"I'm sorry," Rachel said quite simply.

"Why didn't you tell us the truth?" asked Mandy.

"Let me guess," said James, rubbing the toe of his

27

boot backward and forward in the snow. "You didn't tell the truth because that would have meant no guinea pigs. And you wanted the guinea pigs too badly to risk that."

Rachel nodded.

Mandy could see that she was about to start crying again. "It's freezing out here," she said. "Why don't we come inside, and we'll decide what to do."

Rachel gave a shuddering sob and nodded again.

Mandy and James pulled off their boots in the hall while Rachel went to make drinks. The house was quiet except for the sound of clanking mugs coming from the kitchen.

"Do you like hot chocolate?" Rachel asked.

Hot chocolate! Who didn't?

"Mom and Amy are out, so we've got the place to ourselves." Rachel made an attempt at a smile and began to fill the mugs with milk and chocolate powder. She put them into the microwave and switched it on.

"You were right, James," she said at last. "I was just so desperate to look after the guinea pigs that I think I would have said anything to get them. I know it was wrong."

"Why won't your dad let you keep them in the garage?" Mandy asked.

"Because he says he's running a business, not a zoo."

Rachel took the mugs from the microwave and

handed them to Mandy and James. They wrapped their cold hands around the soothing warmth. The hot chocolate was delicious.

"Mmm," said James. "Perfect for a snowy morning."

Rachel smiled.

"Any chance of having another talk with your dad?" Mandy asked doubtfully.

"I've been thinking." Rachel took a slow sip of her chocolate, and Mandy could see her face begin to turn red. "Is there any chance of me helping out at Animal Ark in some way? To show Mom and Dad that I really am serious about animals? They seem to think it's a stage I'm going through and that I'll grow out of it." Rachel turned even redder. She obviously found it very embarrassing to ask.

Mandy smiled. If animals were just a stage, in her own case it was a stage that had lasted a very long time! And she was certain it would last forever.

"I'll talk to Mom and Dad about it," said Mandy. "They'd need to be convinced that you were serious about animals, though, and not just fooling around."

"I *am* serious," said Rachel.

"Good, because animals aren't something you can just stop and start when you feel like it," said Mandy.

"Mandy's right," said James. "You have to be absolutely sure, Rachel."

"I'm absolutely one hundred percent sure," she said firmly.

"Good," said Mandy. "Let's go and have a word with your dad then."

By the time they'd pulled on their boots and coats and walked back over to the garage, Mandy's courage wasn't riding quite so high. Mr. Farmer was a very nice man but he was also a determined one!

He was still doing paperwork in the office when they arrived, and he looked up at them all as they stood nervously in the doorway.

"What's this?" His voice was firm but his eyes were kind. The three friends shuffled their feet and looked at one another, hoping somebody else would have the courage to speak first. At last, Mandy found her voice.

"Mr. Farmer, Rachel's asked if she can come and help out at Animal Ark," she began.

"And?" said Mr. Farmer, raising his eyebrows.

"And I think that's a very good idea," said Mandy, "if it's okay with Mom and Dad. Rachel would learn a lot about caring for animals."

"Please, Dad, say that I can. Please."

Mr. Farmer didn't say anything for a while. Then he said, "I think that might be very good for you. I don't know how good it would be for the animals, though!"

"It would be good for them," said Rachel. "I'd love them."

"It takes a little more than loving, though, Rachel," said Mr. Farmer. "You need some practical skill. It's not enough for me to just love cars if I'm going to do my job; I need to know how to fix them as well."

"I'll teach her everything she needs to know," said Mandy. "I think Rachel really is committed to animals."

"And Johnny Foster's guinea pigs need someone to look after them for the weekend," James said quietly. He was blushing furiously.

"You kids certainly know how to push your luck," said Mr. Farmer. But he was smiling. "Go on then! Go and bring in those animals!"

"Oh, thanks, Dad!" Rachel bent down and gave her father an enormous kiss on his cheek. Mr. Farmer patted her on the arm and grinned from ear to ear.

Then Rachel rushed to follow Mandy and James out of the garage. There was important business to attend to!

They found a quiet place at the back of the garage. It was warm and free from drafts, perfect for guinea pigs.

Rachel carefully took the blankets off the hutch and bent down to open the door. "Aren't they beautiful?" she asked. Her eyes danced and her face filled with love for the little creatures. "I'll look after them very carefully," she said.

Rachel was nervous about lifting the guinea pigs out, so Mandy showed her how to take Brandy from the cage without startling or hurting her. "Now you do it," said Mandy. "And remember to handle her firmly, even though you're being gentle. That way, she'll have confidence in you."

Rachel put her hand under the animal's belly and lifted her out of the cage. Brandy hardly struggled at all and Rachel smiled up at Mandy and James. "That was all right, wasn't it?"

Mandy and James both nodded.

"Now try lifting one of the babies," said James. He took Brandy from Rachel and began to stroke her glossy brown-and-white fur. Soon Brandy was sniffing at James and beginning to explore this new person. James laughed and held out a piece of carrot from the supply that Johnny had left behind. Brandy began to nibble at it hungrily.

"She thinks she might like to come to the Hotel Farmer again," said Mandy with a smile.

Mr. Farmer strolled over to the little group and began to stroke Brandy with one finger. "She has a lovely soft coat," he said.

"Look at this one, Dad." Rachel stood up and Mandy saw that she had one of the babies in her hand. "It was sitting all by itself in the corner of the hutch. It looked so lonely."

The tiny brown-and-white guinea pig nestled in the palm of Rachel's hand while she stroked it gently. Then suddenly, he lifted his head and seemed to look Rachel straight in the eye.

"Hello, little guinea pig," she said. The baby twitched

his whiskers and pushed his nose under Rachel's thumb. "Oh, look, he's hiding. He feels safe in my hand."

"That's the one that Johnny's worried about," said Mandy. "He just sits in a corner and never plays with the others."

"Well, I'm going to give him some special tender loving care," said Rachel, holding the baby close to her face. "I'll soon get him running around."

Mandy and James laughed, and Mandy noticed that Mr. Farmer was smiling quietly to himself. And he was still stroking Brandy!

"These babies are going to need new homes soon," said James.

"Yes, well, this garage might be a temporary shelter for a family of guinea pigs," said Mr. Farmer, "but it's not going to become a permanent home for them. Whoever heard of such a thing? A guinea pig in the garage!"

Mandy was busy telling her parents all about the morning's events. They were sitting around the kitchen table enjoying some delicious homemade vegetable soup. "Just the thing for a cold day," Mandy had said when she saw it.

"The baby's probably all right," said Dr. Emily when Mandy told her about the smallest guinea pig. "It sounds as though it's the runt of the litter, and it's going to have to work a little harder in life. The important thing is to make sure that it gets enough food and drink. If it doesn't perk up within a few days, I'll ask Johnny Foster to bring it in so I can have a look at it."

"Thanks, Mom," said Mandy.

"How were Grandma and Grandpa?" asked Dr. Emily, changing the subject.

Mandy's mouth dropped open and she felt herself go red. "Sorry, Mom! We were so busy sorting out Brandy and her babies, I completely forgot about going to Lilac Cottage. And it took ages walking through the snow."

"I think Grandma and Grandpa will have to grow soft, furry coats and develop wet noses and pleading eyes," said Dr. Adam. "Then Mandy won't forget about them."

"That's not fair, Dad!" Mandy felt terrible. "You know I always go and see Grandma and Grandpa." And Mandy did. Mr. and Mrs. Hope Senior were adored by their granddaughter just as much as they loved her.

"I'm only joking, love." Dr. Adam pulled gently at Mandy's cheek.

Mandy sniffed. "I'll go and see them now. I'll call James and meet him there. We're going sledding up at High Cross Farm."

"It's ages since I've been sledding," Dr. Emily said regretfully. "Can I join you later if there's time?" she asked.

"Of course you can, Mom. That'd be great!" Mandy kissed her mother on the cheek and waved good-bye to her parents.

"Hurricane Mandy's off again," said Dr. Adam, blowing Mandy a kiss.

The snow had stopped when Mandy stepped out of the house. The sky had turned a beautiful shade of blue, and the branches of the trees were black against the skyline. Mandy thought it was perfect, like a painting on a Christmas card.

Just as she reached the gate of Lilac Cottage, she saw James plodding through the snow, leaning forward slightly as he pulled his sled. There was no sign of Blackie; James must have decided not to bring him.

But as her friend came nearer, Mandy realized that she was wrong. Blackie was sitting on the sled, hidden behind his master. He obviously believed in traveling in style! He sat upright on the sled, as stately as a king, while James pulled him along, puffing and panting for breath.

Mandy laughed out loud. Blackie stood up and wagged his tail furiously. He leaped from the sled and tried to jump at her.

Mandy stepped backward so that Blackie's paws simply landed in the snow. James had taught her this to discourage Blackie from jumping up. It wasn't working very well so far!

"You're supposed to say 'down' as well," said James, "to reinforce the message."

"I'm not quite sure how you reinforce messages with Blackie," Mandy said with a grin. "He's absolutely un-trainable."

"He is not!" cried James. "He just needs a little more encouragement than some, that's all."

Blackie wagged his tail in agreement and shot off up Grandma and Grandpa Hope's walkway. He knew from past experience that there was usually something tasty at the other end!

By the time Mandy and James got to the porch, Blackie looked like a huge round snowball.

"I can't take him inside like that," said James. "I'd better tie him to something."

"Tie him to the drainpipe," said Mandy. "Then he can sit on the porch and keep dry."

The door opened and Grandpa stood there beaming at the two of them.

"Hello, Grandpa," said Mandy. "I've come to see if you and Grandma are all right. Mom wondered if you might need something, with all this snow around."

"I see," said Grandma, coming up to the door behind

her husband. "You haven't come to see us for the pleasure of our company then?"

"You know what I mean, Grandma. It's always great
to see you."

And it was. She and James sat in the big kitchen,
drinking hot chocolate and munching on Grandma's
homemade ginger cookies.

"I've just had lunch," said Mandy, "but I can't resist
your cookies, Grandma."

"Best in town," said Grandpa.

"Oh, go on," said Grandma. But Mandy could see that
she was pleased.

"I wish I were still young enough for sledding," said
Grandpa after Mandy had told him the afternoon plans.
"I used to love sledding when I was younger."

"It wasn't that long ago," said Mandy. "I can remember you pulling me along on my sled."

"Yes," said Grandpa, with a twinkle in his eye.

"You can tell your mom that we've got everything we
need," said Grandma.

Mandy grinned. Grandma and Grandpa were very in-
dependent and didn't really need anybody to look after
them. Mandy was glad.

"And here you are, young James," said Grandma.
"Here's a muffin for that beautiful dog of yours."

"It's a bit of a waste, Mrs. Hope," said James. "He'll just gulp it down in one bite."

"Yes, but he'll enjoy it," Grandma said with a smile.

Blackie did enjoy it; at least for the two seconds that it lasted. Mandy and James laughed. Blackie really was a very greedy dog!

Four

The two friends headed off toward the Beacon and High Cross Farm. Here the hills were high and steep, perfect for sledding.

Their friend Lydia Fawcett lived at High Cross Farm. She kept a small herd of goats that produced wonderful milk and cheese. It was a solitary existence, but Lydia loved her farm.

"There's the Beacon," said Mandy.

"Thank goodness for that!" said James. He was puffing and panting, while Blackie still sat elegantly on the back of the sled!

Blackie had provided entertainment for almost the whole of Welford. Everyone who had seen him had smiled at the sight of a big black Labrador gliding along in comfort!

"We'd better pop in and see Lydia, to check that she doesn't mind us using her land," said Mandy.

Lydia didn't. She was sitting by the fire, paying her bills, when they arrived.

"This is paperwork weather," she said. "Nice warm fire and a pile of paperwork; what could be better?"

"Sledding?" suggested Mandy.

Lydia laughed. "Perhaps you're right."

They discussed the coming auction. "We didn't see you at the village hall last night," said Mandy. She knew that Lydia intended to be involved with Save Our Sanctuary.

Lydia glanced out the window. "Can you blame me?"

"No," said Mandy. High Cross Farm was isolated even in the best weather. And wading through deep snow on a dark night was not anyone's idea of fun!

"I'm not sure what I'm going to do for the auction yet," Mandy said, "but I'm sure I'll think of something!"

They thanked Lydia and headed off for the best sledding hill they could find. It was perfect. A smooth, steep slope with very few trees to get in their way.

"The trouble with sledding," said James, "is that coming down the hills is fantastic but it's not much fun going up!"

"We could use a ski lift," said Mandy. "Anyway, at least Blackie's making his own way now."

Blackie was tearing ahead up the hillside, sending sprays of snow flying all around him and barking madly.

Mandy and James laughed. "He'll cause an avalanche if he's not careful," said James.

"At least he doesn't need you to pull him up the hill," said Mandy. "Race you to the bottom!"

"Let's get to the top first!" said James.

At the top of the hill, Blackie tried to get on the sled with James.

"You'll never win with Blackie as passenger," laughed Mandy. She was sitting upright on her sled, ready to start the race.

"And *you'll* never win in that position," said James. "You need to lie flat." He moved Blackie firmly off the sled and lay on his front, facing down the hill. "This is the way to do it."

"We'll see about that!" said Mandy. "On your mark . . . get set . . . *go!*"

At first, James was ahead and Mandy began to wish she'd taken his advice. She leaned backward to see if that helped. It did. She felt the sled gathering speed, bumping over the tufts of grass beneath the snow, the wind whistling past her ears. It was exhilarating! She could hear Blackie barking and James shouting.

And then she was at the bottom. The sled skidded slightly as it hit a bump under the snow, and finally came to a halt in front of a drystone wall.

Mandy looked back up the hill. She grinned as she saw James, desperately trying to catch up, but hindered by Blackie weaving backward and forward in front of the sled!

"My dog," said James, when he finally got to the bottom of the slope, "needs some serious training."

"Really?" said Mandy. "I hadn't noticed."

James scowled at her and Mandy laughed. "It's no use blaming Blackie just because you lost the race!"

James threw a pretend punch and they began to pull their sleds back up the hill. There was no point trying to race with Blackie around; they'd just have to go in for some straightforward sledding.

"Let me give Blackie a ride," said Mandy. She patted the sled. "Here, Blackie. Come!"

Blackie, always obedient when he sensed a treat in store, jumped onto Mandy's sled and sat in front of her.

He loved it! The Labrador's ears blew backward in the wind and he looked as if he were flying! When they reached the bottom of the hill he stayed on the sled, ob-

viously hoping to be pulled back up. Mandy shrieked with laughter. "Not a chance, you lazy thing," she told him. "I'm not as soft as your master."

Blackie did pretty well with rides. When he wasn't allowed one, he ran down the hillside alongside the sleds, barking and causing mini-avalanches.

Blackie was riding in front of Mandy when Mandy noticed the Hopes' Land Rover pull up and Dr. Emily climb out.

Mandy waved. "Up here!" she called.

Blackie had spotted Dr. Emily, too. He was very fond of her. He leaped from the sled and ran off down the hillside. Unfortunately, his sudden movement unbalanced the sled and before Mandy knew what was happening, she, the sled, and Blackie were sailing through the air. They landed more or less together in a big heap.

Mandy wasn't hurt but Blackie gave a sudden yelp. She sat up, dazed with shock. Blackie was yelping loudly and trying to limp across the snow toward James. James, his face anxious with worry, ran toward his beloved pet. Dr. Emily sprinted toward them.

"Mandy, are you all right?" she called.

"I'm fine." Mandy shook her head and straightened her arms and legs. She was perfectly okay. But Blackie wasn't.

She pulled herself to her feet and ran over to the little group huddled together in the snow. Blackie was still yelping. Mandy felt a lump at the back of her throat.

Dr. Emily ran her hands over one of Blackie's front legs.

"Is it broken?" asked James, his voice unsteady.

"I'm not sure," said Dr. Emily. "I'll have to get him back to the clinic. Can you help me to get him to lie down on the sled?"

Between them, James and Dr. Emily lifted Blackie carefully onto James's sled. Blackie yelped as they moved him, but his yelps subsided to whimpers as he lay on the sled, being pulled toward the Animal Ark Land Rover.

They weren't able to open the gate at the bottom of the field. Mandy, James, and Blackie had lifted their sleds over the wall. But with Blackie on the sled, it would be difficult.

"James and I will lift Blackie and the sled so that they're resting on top of the gate," Dr. Emily explained. "Then, Mandy, you hold it balanced there while James and I go over the wall and around to the other side. Then you and I can lift it down between us, James."

They nodded. James was on the verge of tears.

But the plan worked perfectly, and before long Blackie was installed in the back of the Land Rover with James sitting beside him. The dog had stopped whimpering now, but he was unusually quiet.

Back at the clinic, James helped Dr. Emily to lift Blackie onto the examination table. She examined his leg again.

"It's really too swollen for me to know for sure whether there's a break or not. I'm going to have to X-ray the leg."

"Can I stay with him?" asked James.

"Not while I take the X ray. We'll all have to keep clear of that, because too much exposure to X rays can be dangerous," Dr. Emily explained. "And I'll have to give Blackie an anesthetic, too."

"Why?" asked James.

"Because I need to have the leg in a particular position so that I can get the exact picture I want from the X ray. Even the best-trained dog in the world will move if it's not under anesthesia, and then you don't get the right picture."

James nodded. "And nobody can stay to hold the dog in position because that would mean being exposed to the X ray?"

"That's right, James." said Dr. Emily. "But before we start, you'd better give your parents a call for permission to go ahead with the treatment."

"Shall I do that?" asked Mandy. "Then you can stay with Blackie."

"Thanks, Mandy," said James. He felt a little calmer now because of Dr. Emily's reassuring manner and because Blackie was calmer, too. James stroked Blackie while he waited for Mandy.

"That's fine," said Mandy, coming back into the clinic. "Your mom's on her way down, too."

James nodded. He held on to Blackie and stroked his head while Dr. Emily gave him the anesthetic injection. As soon as the Labrador was asleep, which was only a matter of seconds, Mandy and James went into the waiting room to wait for the X ray results.

When Dr. Emily came in a little while later, she was smiling. "Good news, James. The leg's not broken, just badly bruised. He'll need to go easy for a few days until the swelling goes down, and then he'll be as right as rain."

Tears began to trickle down James's face. "I'm just so relieved," he said when Dr. Emily put her arm around him.

"I know you are," she said. "Come and see Blackie in a few minutes. He'll be awake by then and pleased to see you."

James smiled through the tears and nodded.

Mandy found tears on her own face, too. She loved all animals but some were extra-special. Blackie was one of the extra-special ones. It was easy to imagine how poor James must be feeling.

A minute later, James's mother had joined them in the waiting room. She gave James a quick pat on the shoulder. "He's going to be fine, James."

James nodded. "It really hurt him. I was sure the leg was broken."

"Well, it's not, so we must be thankful for that."

"You just need to keep him quiet for a few days and he'll be fine," said Dr. Emily, coming back into the room. "His own common sense will tell him to keep off the leg while it's still bruised."

"I don't know how you can refer to Blackie and common sense in the same breath, Emily," said Mrs. Hunter.

Even James laughed, and both he and Blackie looked a little brighter when Mandy waved good-bye to them.

Back in the kitchen, Dr. Emily made a pot of tea and toasted muffins. Dr. Adam came in from a visit and sniffed happily at the delicious smell.

"Just what I need after wading through the snow to a lambing," he said.

"Everything okay?" asked Mandy.

"I think so," said Dad as he sat down at the table and helped himself to a muffin. "The farmer was being cautious because they were early. They should be fine, though."

Mandy told her father about Blackie.

"It's a good thing you were there, Emily."

"Well, actually, if I hadn't been there it might never have happened." Dr. Emily explained about Blackie jumping off the sled to meet her. "And I never even managed to get my sled out of the Land Rover!"

"Never mind, Mom. The snow will still be around tomorrow."

"It will be around for a lot longer than that, if you ask me," said Dr. Adam. "It's just started snowing again."

"I need to get down to see Rachel Farmer," said Mandy. "James was supposed to come with me, but he probably won't feel like it now that Blackie's been injured."

"I don't think you should go out again tonight," said Mom. "Especially now that it's started snowing again. Give Rachel a call and tell her you'll see her tomorrow."

"Okay," Mandy agreed. She was glad Mom had said that. For once she felt more like curling up by the fire than going out.

Thinking of Rachel reminded Mandy about Johnny Foster's guinea pigs. She began to tell Mom and Dad the whole story. Then she remembered that she'd promised to ask her parents if Rachel could help out at Animal Ark for a while.

"I don't see why not," said Dr. Emily.

"As long as she's properly supervised and realizes that it's a responsible job," said Dad. "Even if you're only sweeping out the bedding."

"Oh, I think she does," said Mandy. "I've had a talk with her and explained all of that."

"Well, let her try then," said Dr. Adam.

"Five or six weeks should be enough to let her see what working with animals is all about," said Dr. Emily. "I'll draw up a proper schedule and she can start on Monday."

Five

"I'd better make a run for the clinic," said Mom after breakfast the following morning. "The waiting room's starting to fill up already." She pushed her chair back from the table. "All those cancelled appointments are coming in now that the roads are passable."

Mandy looked out the window. The snow was still thick and the temperature was around freezing; the snow was going to be there for quite some time yet. But the snowplows and sanders had been out, and Mandy could see black ribbons of road twisting across the valley. There'd be school on Monday unless it snowed again.

The waiting room was nearly full as Mandy went through into the residential unit. Simon was already there, holding something small and furry in his arms.

"Let me see," said Mandy.

Simon handed her a tiny mongrel puppy, all black except for a patch of white across his nose and one of his paws.

"Oh, you darling." Mandy rubbed her cheek against the top of his head. "Oh, Simon, he's so gorgeous I could eat him!"

"I wouldn't recommend it," said Simon, grinning. "I don't think the owner would be too pleased."

"What's the matter with him?"

"He had an argument with a motorcycle."

Mandy's eyes widened. "But he looks all right," she said.

"The bike wasn't moving at the time," said Simon. "It belongs to his owner, and it fell on top of him. We've given him a full examination and he seems to be fine, but the owner's terribly nervous; he wants us to keep him under observation for a day or two."

"I'll observe him for you," Mandy said with a grin. "He can come sledding with me and James."

"I don't think that's quite the sort of observation the owner had in mind," said Simon. "I think he was after something a bit quieter. And after what happened to

Blackie I don't think I'd be inclined to let a puppy go sledding with you."

"You're probably right," said Mandy.

Mandy gave the puppy a final pat and began to clear out the bedding from two cages that had been recently occupied but were now empty. There was only one other occupant, and that was a standard poodle by the name of Woolly. She'd had quite a serious operation and was staying at Animal Ark for a few days to recover.

"Could you exercise Woolly for me?" asked Simon. "I think she's up to a short stroll now. The roads are clear, but don't let her get in any snow."

Mandy fetched Woolly's leash and dressed herself up in boots and a jacket. She'd take Woolly down to the end of the road and back, not too far for her first outing.

"Come on, Woolly. Time for a walk." The big black poodle came hesitantly out of the cage and then gave a big yawn and stretched her legs. Her head came up to Mandy's hips as she leaned her weight against Mandy.

Simon laughed. "She looks as though she's about to drop off to sleep," he said.

"Poor old thing," said Mandy. "I think she's still feeling a bit woozy from her operation."

"She'll be fine," said Simon. "Just keep an eye on her."

"I will," said Mandy, closing the door behind her.

She had reached the bottom of the road and was

about to turn around again when she saw Rachel
Farmer. Mandy waved and called to her.

"How are you getting along with the guinea pigs?" she
asked.

"Fine," said Rachel. "I've fed them this morning and
given them clean water. And, of course, I've had a cuddle with every one of them!"

Mandy laughed.

"I feed the quiet one when he's out of the cage by himself. I've been handling him a lot."

"Good for you," said Mandy. "You'll do him a world of
good. You'll have to become a guinea pig foster parent!"

"I'd rather have one of my own," Rachel said ruefully.
"What a gorgeous dog," she said, suddenly noticing
Woolly.

Mandy explained about Woolly's operation.

"Could I walk her for a bit?"

Mandy was reluctant. "I think she's been far enough,
Rachel, I don't want to overtire her."

"Just down to the signpost?"

Woolly seemed to think it was a good idea. She
wagged her tail for the first time since her operation
and sniffed eagerly at Rachel's hand.

"She likes me," said Rachel with a big smile on her face.

"Go on then," said Mandy, smiling, too. "Just as far as
the signpost."

Mandy watched the pair of them. Rachel spoke to Woolly as they walked, and the dog really did seem to like the girl. Woolly's ears had pricked up and she walked with a more lively step.

But then Woolly quickened her pace and broke into a trot. Rachel increased her own speed to keep up with the dog, and within a few seconds, the pair of them were running.

"Stop!" called Mandy. "Rachel, stop!"

Either Rachel didn't hear or she couldn't stop. Mandy began to run after them, her heart beating with fear for Woolly's safety. She should never have let Rachel walk Woolly; the girl had no real experience with animals.

Mandy had almost caught up with them when she saw Rachel skid on a patch of ice and come crashing down onto the hard surface of the road. Woolly, sensing freedom, cantered off toward Welford.

"Oh, no!" Mandy gasped. She began to run even faster. If anything happened to Woolly, she'd never forgive herself. More important, Woolly's owner would probably never forgive her, either! Mom and Dad would get into trouble, too. Woolly's owner would probably tell everyone, and Animal Ark would go out of business!

To Mandy's relief, Woolly began to slow down. But then the big black poodle squeezed through a fence into an adjacent field. There she lay on her back with her legs in the air, squirming and wriggling with delight in the cold, wet snow.

"Woolly!" Mandy made a final bolt toward the runaway dog.

Woolly's tongue was hanging out of the side of her mouth. It looked as if she were laughing!

"You might as well laugh, you naughty dog," said Mandy. But she couldn't help smiling, too, as she caught hold of the dog's leash. Woolly certainly seemed to have made a very good recovery from her operation! All Mandy had to do now was get Woolly back to Animal Ark and explain to Simon about her wet coat. She was not looking forward to it.

When Mandy got back onto the road, she saw Rachel walking toward them, rubbing her elbow.

"I really hurt myself," she said. "I thought I'd broken my arm."

"What about poor old Woolly?" said Mandy. "She could have been run over. And she's soaking wet. It's not going to do her a lot of good after a big operation, you know."

"I know. I'm sorry, Mandy." Rachel hung her head and looked thoroughly miserable. "I suppose you think I'm no good with animals now."

"No, of course I don't think that." Mandy had calmed down after her shock, and she began to feel sorry for Rachel; she was obviously very upset.

"The problem was that you started to run when she did," said Mandy. "If you'd stuck to your guns and refused to run, then Woolly would have gotten the message."

"I'll try to remember that next time. Don't tell your mom and dad, will you?"

"I don't know," said Mandy. "You need to take more care in the future."

"I will, I promise. Can I still come to Animal Ark on Monday?"

Mandy nodded.

"Thanks, Mandy. See you then." And Rachel left, running off toward the village.

Mandy sighed and shook her head. She hoped having Rachel at Animal Ark was going to turn out all right.

Meanwhile, she had some explaining to do. She'd better get on with it!

Simon's face was serious when she told him what had happened.

"You really shouldn't have let anybody else take her," he said. "It could have ended much worse than it did."

"I know." Mandy felt tears prick at her eyes. She really didn't need Simon to tell her how careless she'd been. But she supposed she deserved the lecture.

"Rub her down until she's absolutely dry," said Simon. "And take care around the operation site; don't pull the skin."

Mandy did as she was told. She didn't stop toweling the dog until she was completely dry. She didn't dare take any risks now.

"Give her plenty of bedding," said Simon, "and cover her with a blanket. We need to make sure she doesn't get cold."

Mandy did as she was told and then took herself off to the kitchen for a bag of chips.

"You look as though you've lost your best friend," said Dr. Adam, coming into the kitchen.

Before she knew what was happening, she had her head buried in her hands and the tears were flowing through her fingers.

"What's this all about?" Dr. Adam pulled his chair up next to her and put his arm around her shoulder. Mandy couldn't say anything for a while, but at last she was able to tell her father what had happened. She felt so bad about it that it was a relief to tell him.

"But, please, don't tell me how stupid I've been because I know."

"I wouldn't dream of it," Dr. Adam said gently. "You took a risk, and it turned out badly. You'll know better next time. Shall we go and take a look at Woolly now and check that she's okay?"

In the residential unit, Simon took one look at Mandy's red eyes and said nothing.

Mandy and Dr. Adam bent down to look into Woolly's cage. She was sleeping peacefully, as if exhausted by her morning's excursion.

Dr. Adam examined the poodle carefully. He took her temperature. "That's fine," he said. "Absolutely normal. I don't think there's anything to worry about, Mandy. We'll keep a close eye on her, of course."

Mandy nodded, relieved that Woolly seemed none the worse for her adventure.

"I'm going to see Rachel now," she said.

"Is that the girl who's coming to help out? The one who let go of Woolly?"

"Yes," said Mandy.

Dr. Adam looked thoughtful. "She'll have to be a little more careful in the future. You know that, don't you?"

Mandy nodded. "So does she. But she's so desperate to keep one of Brandy's babies that she'll do anything to try to persuade her father. I want to go and put her mind at ease about Woolly."

Mandy found Rachel in the garage with the guinea pigs. Rachel held the tiny one in the palm of her hand. She was talking gently to it and stroking it with one finger. She blushed when she looked up and saw Mandy.

"I suppose you've come to tell me that I can't come to Animal Ark on Monday."

"No, of course not, Rachel. I've come to tell you that Woolly's fine and Dad doesn't think she's been hurt."

Rachel gave a little smile. She still looked upset.

"Don't worry," said Mandy. "You're forgiven."

Rachel's smile broadened. "Really?" she asked.

"Really," said Mandy.

"Look, Mandy. Let me show you what Hero can do." Her face was shining now with relief and excitement.

"Who's Hero?" Mandy asked.

"The smallest baby," said Rachel. "He might be tiny, but he's a hero. You wait and see."

There was a square of old carpeting beside the guinea pigs' hutch. Rachel scattered a few sunflower seeds across it and placed Hero carefully at the edge. She held her hands close to him so that he couldn't escape.

Hero nosed around the carpet, his whiskers twitching. At last he found the first sunflower seed, which he ate. He then began to look for the second one.

"Isn't he clever?" said Rachel. "I've been training him nearly all morning."

"He's brilliant," said Mandy. She watched as Hero

eventually found and ate all four sunflower seeds. When they were gone, he pattered over to Rachel and looked up at her with bright black eyes.

Rachel picked him up and he snuggled into the palm of her hand. Then he pushed his nose under her thumb and went to sleep!

"Just look at that," said Mandy. "He's a real cutie, isn't he?"

"He's the one I love best," said Rachel. She picked Hero up and held him close to her chest. "He knows me now," she said.

"Who knows you now?"

The two girls turned at the sound of Mr. Farmer's voice. He was strolling toward them, smiling broadly. Mandy thought he knew exactly who Rachel was talking about!

"Hero, of course," said Rachel.

"I think I'm the hero around here, having guinea pigs in the garage," said Rachel's dad. "My men will think I've gone crazy."

But Mr. Farmer bent down and took Hero from Rachel's hand. He stroked him gently. "I like Hero very much," he said, "but I think Brandy's my favorite. She's got such a beautiful coat."

"Hero's coat will be just as beautiful when he grows up," said Rachel. "He needs a really good home with somebody who'll look after him properly and make sure he gets everything he needs. Then he'll have the glossiest coat in the whole country."

Mr. Farmer laughed. He seemed as fond of guinea pigs as Rachel was.

Mandy was thrilled. Perhaps Hero wouldn't have to look very far to find a really good home!

Six

Mandy called for James on the way to Grandma and Grandpa's house. They were going sledding again but this time without Blackie, who was nursing his bruised leg.

"He's a lot better this morning," said James. "He's still limping around and he's a little reluctant to put any weight on his leg, but I think he's healing."

Mandy smiled with relief as she pushed open the gate to Lilac Cottage.

"Hello, you two," said Grandma. "Come on in."

"If you can get in," said Grandpa. "We're knee-deep in

muffins at the moment. And bread and cakes. You name it and Grandma's made it."

"I've offered to bake bread and cakes for the auction," Grandma explained. "And your dad tells me he's giving a talk on animal welfare."

"I didn't know that," said Mandy.

"You do now," Grandpa said with a grin.

"I'm looking forward to the auction," said Grandma. "It should be a good evening."

"Yes, it should," said James. "Do you remember the last auction we went to, Mandy?"

Mandy smiled and nodded. She and James had helped out old Mr. Matthews on his dairy farm when he had become ill, and he had named one of his new calves after Mandy. His farm had been saved at the last minute at an exciting auction.

"Do you two think you'll do anything for the auction?" asked Grandpa.

"I'm going to offer to do dog walking," said Mandy. "I think I'll offer my services as a dog walker for a week."

"If you get fifty-two offers that means you'll be walking dogs for a year," said James, grinning at the thought. "Your legs will get shorter and shorter."

"Don't worry, Mandy," said Grandma. "Your services go to the highest bidder, not to everyone who bids."

"That's a relief!" said Mandy.

"I think I might offer basic computer lessons," said James.

"I should think you'd have plenty of customers," said Grandpa. "But I'm afraid to say that I won't be one of them. I think the computer age has passed me by."

"I've already started to stock the freezer," said Grandma, "but there's still a lot more to do." She got up from the table and began to clear away the pots.

"We'd better go, too, if we want to get any sledding in before it gets dark!" said James.

"It's a shame you've got to go back to school today," said Dr. Emily on Monday morning.

"Perhaps it'll snow again," said Mandy.

But it didn't. It was dark when she arrived home from school, and she had to help James take Brandy and Hero back to Johnny Foster. Then Rachel was coming to help at Animal Ark. There'd be no time for sledding!

When she and James arrived at the garage, they found Rachel already there, giving each of the guinea pigs a last cuddle.

"I'm really going to miss them," she said miserably.

Mandy lifted Brandy from the hutch and James was already stroking one of the babies. "Have you said anything to your dad about keeping Hero?" she asked.

Rachel shook her head. "I don't dare. I'm just so scared he'll say no."

"You've looked after them really well," said James. "I think Johnny will be very pleased they've been so well cared for."

"James is right," said Mandy. "And if you don't ask your father if you can have Hero, then he won't have the chance to say yes."

Rachel nodded. "I know you're right; it's just so difficult."

"What's so difficult?" Mr. Farmer's voice came booming across from the other side of the garage. If there were no noisy jobs going on in the garage, the big, echoey space carried every word quite clearly. No wonder Mr. Farmer seemed to have such sharp ears!

The little group stood stock still. Rachel had turned red and Mandy felt her heart hammering. It was now or never!

"We were just saying what a good job Rachel's done looking after the guinea pigs, Mr. Farmer. Especially with Hero," said Mandy.

"Yes, she really does seem to have the knack," James added.

Rachel just looked at her father with pleading eyes.

"Do I get the impression that you three are trying to twist my arm?" Mr. Farmer's voice was gentle. "She has done a good job; she's a good girl. But my answer's still no. I'm sorry, but that's the way it is."

Mr. Farmer turned and walked away. Mandy's heart sank with disappointment, and tears trickled slowly down Rachel's face.

Mandy put her arm around the girl's shoulder. "I'm really sorry, Rachel. You deserve to have a pet."

"Yes, you do," James added kindly. "But we'd better get these guinea pigs home to Johnny now."

Brandy and the babies were put back into the hutch. "Good-bye," Rachel whispered. She covered the hutch carefully with the old blankets, and then the three friends lifted it onto Mandy's sled.

Poor Rachel, thought Mandy.

Although the roads had been cleared, most of the pavements were still covered with snow, so it was fairly easy to pull the sled and the hutch along. They took turns and it wasn't long before they reached Johnny's house.

But when they got there, they found that the house was deserted. Although it was dark, the curtains were still open, and there wasn't a light on in the house!

"They were supposed to be getting back late last night," said Rachel. "I didn't see Johnny at school today, but I just thought I'd missed him in the playground."

"Well, there's certainly no one here now," said Mandy. "Perhaps we should just put the hutch back in the shed. They're sure to be back before too long."

"But what if they're not?" said Rachel. "Then the guinea pigs will be all alone with no one to look after them. I'm not going to leave them here by themselves."

"I think Rachel's right," said James. "They may have

been delayed for some reason. I don't think we can risk it."

Mandy nodded. "Okay. But look, Rachel's coming to Animal Ark with me anyway, and as far as Johnny knows the guinea pigs are still there. I forgot to call him at his grandmother's — what with Blackie's accident and everything — so he doesn't know that Rachel's been looking after them. Maybe he'll go to Animal Ark to collect them. Come on, let's go home and see. We'll take the guinea pigs with us."

The two girls waved good-bye to James and headed on to Animal Ark. But when they arrived, there was no sign of Johnny.

"Mandy, message for you!" called Jean as they went into reception.

Mandy took the piece of paper and read it quickly. "It's from Johnny," she told Rachel. "Apparently his grandmother's ill, so they won't be back for a while. He doesn't know how long."

Mandy looked anxiously at Rachel's face. But Rachel was beaming! "That means I'll be able to look after the guinea pigs until he gets back. It might be ages!" she said.

Mandy couldn't help smiling at the girl's excited face. But deep down she was worried. Rachel already loved the guinea pigs, especially Hero. The longer she kept

them, the harder it was going to be for her to part with
them.

"Come on, Rachel. We'll put Brandy and her babies
into the shed while we do the chores."

Mandy opened the door to the shed and switched on
the light. Between them, she and Rachel lifted the
guinea pigs and put them on top of an old table.

"They'll be okay there for a while," said Mandy.

Rachel stood back and admired the little animals
scurrying around the hutch. "Shall I show you how
Hero eats out of my hand?" she asked.

Mandy nodded as Rachel opened the hutch door. The
baby guinea pigs all scurried toward Rachel's hand, but
to Mandy's astonishment, Hero nosed his way between
his brothers and sisters and came to sit in Rachel's
palm.

"Look," Rachel whispered. Her face glowed as she
lifted Hero out of the hutch.

"He's certainly getting over his shyness," Mandy said.

Rachel smiled. "I've spent so much time with him that
he really knows me now. But just watch this, Mandy."

Rachel placed a sunflower seed on the tip of Hero's
quivering nose. He moved quickly so that it fell into
Rachel's hand, but within a second he dived for the seed
and began to eat it.

Then Hero lifted his head and looked around as if to

say, "Any more?" When he saw that there wasn't, he tucked his head under Rachel's thumb once again and went to sleep.

Mandy and Rachel laughed. "I can see he's making quite a habit of sleeping under your thumb," Mandy said.

"Yes, he likes it there," said Rachel. "You know, Mandy, if I could have Hero, it'd be great."

Mandy nodded. "I know I'd love to have a horse, a dog, a cat, rabbits, guinea pigs, hamsters, a donkey, a couple of goats. . . ." Her voice trailed off as she tried to imagine this blissful existence.

"Oh, my!" said a voice beyond the shed door. "I think all of Welford's sick and ailing animals are quite enough to cope with for the moment."

Dr. Adam put his head around the door and grinned at the two girls. "I take it this is Rachel," he said.

Mandy introduced them.

"Welcome on board, Rachel. If you remember to do exactly as Mandy tells you and not to do anything that you haven't been told, then you should have a happy time and learn a lot." Dr. Adam smiled. "I'm just off to deliver some pups who don't want to be born. See you later." Dr. Adam waved and was gone.

Rachel looked after him, her face pink with excitement. "Can you imagine that? Delivering puppies! I can't wait until I'm a vet."

"I know the feeling," said Mandy. "Meanwhile we have to be happy with the routine jobs — like feeding and cleaning out the cages."

The two girls worked side by side. Mandy introduced Rachel to Simon. "Is there anything special you want us to do?" she said.

"No, just the usual things tonight," said Simon.

Woolly and the little puppy were still in their cages. "I thought these two would be gone by now," said Mandy.

"Woolly's going in the morning, and the puppy's owner is ill himself now. He's asked us to hang on to him for a day or two longer."

"We'll be turning into a boarding kennel before you know it," said Mandy.

Rachel was scratching Woolly's nose through the mesh of the cage. "She seems fine," she said softly.

"She's absolutely fine," Mandy said. "I think she really enjoyed her roll in the snow!"

"Look at that little puppy. It's sad to see him all alone like that." Rachel's face suddenly grew serious.

Mandy took the puppy from the cage and let Rachel hold him. His black ears flopped almost to his jaw, and his big brown eyes were shiny and wide. "Oh, he's beautiful. He's just beautiful."

Mandy grinned. She was enjoying showing Rachel around because Rachel enjoyed it so much herself; she really was crazy about animals.

"He seems so lonely, though," said Rachel. "He looks as though he needs his mother."

"I think he's been away from his mother for quite a few weeks now," said Mandy. "But I know what you mean. It is sad to see him all by himself. Would you like to clean out his cage and feed him?"

Rachel looked as though it were her birthday and Christmas all rolled into one. "Would I!" she said, her face glowing with pleasure.

Mandy soon discovered that it was actually more work having someone help. You had to stop and show them every single thing that they had to do. There were lots of things that Mandy was so familiar with that she hardly thought about them. It was not the same with Rachel, though.

When Mandy asked her to change some old bedding and wash down the floor, she forgot to mention that she should use disinfectant. Rachel didn't know, of course, and had just used plain water. So Mandy had to wipe down the floor again, this time using the right cleaner.

"We have to be so careful to avoid infection passing from one animal to another," she explained to Rachel. "It would be dreadful if an animal came in with one problem and went home with another. That's why we always use disinfectant."

But Rachel was a quick learner, and Mandy soon realized that she had only to explain something once for Rachel to get it right the next time around. She really was doing very well.

"Thanks very much for your help, Rachel," said Simon after all the chores were finished. "I can see you're going to be a real asset over the next few weeks."

Rachel beamed with pleasure. She was still too shy in front of Simon to say anything in return, but both he and Mandy realized how delighted she was.

"We'd better get those guinea pigs back to the garage," said Mandy. "If we don't go now, I'll be late for supper, and I'm starving!"

It was easier pulling the sled downhill into Welford than it had been the other way around, and they were back at the garage in just a short while.

Rachel hesitated at the entrance to the huge garage. Bright lights blazed from inside and there was a loud banging of metal. Obviously, Mr. Farmer and his men were busy!

"I hope Dad won't mind the guinea pigs coming back for a while," she said. "He thought he'd gotten rid of them today."

"I'm sure he won't mind," said Mandy, remembering Mr. Farmer's gentle face as he stroked the guinea pigs. "I think you're meant to have a guinea pig in your garage!"

Seven

After leaving Rachel at the garage, Mandy went home and phoned Betty Hilder at the animal sanctuary. The auction was taking place the following evening, and it reminded her that she hadn't visited the sanctuary for a while.

Betty was pleased to hear from her and invited her to visit the sanctuary after school the next day. "There should be time before the auction," she said.

"Can I bring a friend along, too?" Mandy asked. "She's crazy about animals and she's helping out at Animal Ark for a while."

"Of course," said Betty. "I look forward to meeting her."

Mandy and Rachel were coming home on the bus together, ready to get off at the stop nearest the animal sanctuary.

"I've never seen an animal sanctuary before," said Rachel. "What's it like?"

"It's quite a big place," said Mandy, "with a paddock and kennels and all sorts of cages for all sorts of animals. James and I found a baby owl in the woods once and took it to the sanctuary."

"What happened to it?" Rachel asked.

"Betty looked after him until he was better, and then he was sent to a special rehabilitation center so that he could be released into the wild again."

Rachel smiled. "You do have an exciting life, Mandy," she said.

The bus pulled up at their stop and as they got off, they felt the full force of the wind howling across the fields. It whipped the snow across their legs and faces. Mandy shivered and pulled her jacket more tightly around her.

Betty Hilder always dressed practically in jeans and a sweater. When she opened the door in answer to Mandy's knock, she smiled and asked them to come in.

"It's lovely to see the pair of you. And especially nice to meet you, Rachel. I'll just put my coat on and I'll be right there."

"Come and see Rusty first," said Betty, as she stepped outside. "Rusty was rummaging in a garbage pail in the middle of the night, when someone found him with an old can stuck to the end of his nose. It was wedged so tightly they couldn't get it off, so they brought him here to the sanctuary."

"A fox!" Mandy exclaimed as they bent down to look into one of the outside cages. "I should have guessed."

"He's so beautiful," said Rachel, her voice just a whisper. "I've never seen a real, live fox."

"He's a beauty, isn't he?" said Betty.

He certainly was! The fox's fur shone a deep, rusty red in the light from the outside spotlight. He crouched in the corner of his cage, his nose twitching, suspicious of them all. Betty had managed to get the can off, but Mandy could see that it had made a long gash along his nose.

"I'd love to pet him," said Rachel.

"I don't think he'd like the idea of that too much," said Betty. "And we don't want him to, either. I'll be releasing him back into the wild in a day or two, and if I'd tamed him, he wouldn't be able to cope. He has to fend for himself."

Rachel nodded. "I never thought about that," she said.

Betty smiled. "There's a lot to learn about animals. You have to make sure you learn as much as you can if you want to be really kind to them. And that sometimes means not doing the things you'd like to do, like petting them. You have to put their needs first."

"I don't think I'll ever learn it all," said Rachel with a sigh.

Betty laughed. "Don't worry, Rachel. Nobody ever learns it all. Just so long as you keep on trying."

They walked around the rest of the sanctuary. There were two dogs, a magpie, a hedgehog, a litter of kittens that had been left by the main road in danger of being run over, and an elderly goat that was living out the rest of his days at the sanctuary.

As they walked, Betty explained the latest situation at the animal sanctuary. "It's not a major crisis or anything, just routine maintenance such as fencing, and enough money to buy food and medical supplies. You'd be surprised at how expensive all those things can be."

Mandy nodded. In fact, she did have some idea through living at Animal Ark. The difference was that most of Animal Ark's clients paid for any treatment and medicines they had. The Hopes made a living and Animal Ark was a proper business; Betty Hilder relied on donations and struggled to survive.

They were approaching the paddock when Mandy noticed a dark shape in the corner; it took her only a second or two to realize what it was: Bubbles, the black Shetland pony, was almost invisible in the dark.

The little pony came trotting over to them when he heard their footsteps.

"Hello, Bubbles," said Mandy. "I haven't got anything for you, I'm afraid."

The pony nuzzled each of them in turn. Rachel laughed. "Look, he's pushing his nose into my pocket," she said.

Mandy shrieked with laughter as Bubbles nosed around Rachel's pocket and then lifted his head, looking distinctly disappointed!

"You old rogue," said Betty, laughing. "I'm afraid he's a bit spoiled. I should have tried to find a home for him ages ago, but I'm afraid my soft heart got in the way. I just can't bear to part with him now. I regard him as my own pet."

"I don't blame you," said Mandy, stroking the pony's soft neck.

Betty held out a piece of apple for Bubbles, and he took it immediately. "See what I mean? He knows he's always going to get something from me!"

The two girls laughed.

"I'm sorry, Betty, but we should be going," said Mandy. "Otherwise, we'll be late for the auction."

"Me, too," said Betty. "And as the animal sanctuary's the reason for it all, I suppose I should change into something a bit nicer than these baggy old clothes!"

Betty waved good-bye to the two girls as they headed for the bus stop.

"Do you think I could volunteer to look after some small animals for the auction?" asked Rachel as the bus drew up beside them.

"You'd better ask your dad first. You've had enough trouble already; you don't want any more."

Mandy walked home thoughtfully after saying good-bye to Rachel at the bus stop. She hoped Mr. Farmer would let Rachel take care of somebody's pet; it would give her more experience with small animals and she'd be very good at it!

Later that evening, as the Hopes were getting ready to go to the auction, there was a phone call for Mandy. She could hear Rachel's excited voice on the other end of the line even before she put the receiver to her ear!

"Dad says I can offer to look after some small animals for the auction! And guess what? He's coming to the auction with me to offer a car repair! Isn't that great?"

"It's fantastic!" said Mandy. "You can tell your dad's really kind just by looking at him, even though he doesn't always let you have what you want."

Rachel agreed. "He's great, my dad. See you later."

"Are you coming, Mandy? We're centrally heating the whole of Welford!" called Dr. Adam from the open back door.

"Sorry, Dad!" Mandy grabbed her coat and rushed off after her parents.

The village hall had been set up with rows of chairs, and it was so full that Mandy thought some people might have to stand. She spotted James and Rachel waving to her from some seats near the front.

"Saved you one," said James as Mandy joined them.

"Thanks, James." Mandy sat on the hard wooden seat next to her friend. "How's Blackie?"

"He's much better, thanks. I'm just trying to keep him off that leg. But it's hard work. You know what he's like!" Mandy nodded. James peered at his program. "Rachel, it says late entries can be registered with the auctioneer up until seven-thirty."

"I'd better go and tell my dad," Rachel said. "Then we can both go and register."

Mandy and James went to register, too. Julian Hardy, landlord of the Fox and Goose and special auctioneer for the evening, was writing down the details.

As Mandy walked back to her seat, she looked around the room and waved to a dozen people or more. Everyone knew everyone in Welford; that was one of the best things about living in a village. She gave a special wave when she saw Grandma and Grandpa sitting next to her mom and dad.

She squeezed between the rows of chairs to get back to her seat, followed by James and Rachel.

Mr. Hardy was a good auctioneer; he kept the pace of the auction moving quickly and was able to crack a joke every now and then, usually about the person whose services were being auctioned. As the evening progressed, everyone was in a very good mood and having a great time.

Then James's turn came. Mandy saw her friend blush as he heard Mr. Hardy read out his name.

"Mr. James Hunter is offering a series of six lessons in basic computing. I think we all know young Mr. Hunter, don't we? He's the one with Blackie, the best-trained dog in Welford."

The audience laughed out loud and James was laughing, too; but his face was as red as a beet!

Five minutes later, James was blushing with pleasure, not embarrassment. Someone had offered twenty-five dollars for his computer lessons!

Mandy craned her neck to see who the lucky bidder was. She nudged James excitedly. "It's Jean Knox!" she whispered. "You'll have some fun there, James, if she's as scatterbrained with computers as she is with everything else."

Jean already used the computer at Animal Ark, so Mandy didn't really think she was going to be as bad as all that. "She probably just wants to brush up on her skills," she whispered again.

Mrs. Ponsonby bid twenty dollars for Mandy to walk her two dogs for a week. Both of her dogs were rather spoiled — a Pekingese called Pandora and a mongrel called Toby.

"Lucky old you," grinned James.

"Yes, but twenty dollars for the sanctuary — that's amazing!"

Mandy was still smiling when she noticed Betty Hilder a couple of rows behind them; Betty looked almost overwhelmed at the success of the auction.

Mandy turned to the front again as she heard Julian Hardy bang his auctioneer's hammer. "And now, ladies and gentlemen, for our very last item. This is offered by the best car mechanic in Welford: Rachel Farmer."

There was more good-natured laughter, and Rachel turned pink, but not as pink as James had!

It wasn't long before someone had offered five dollars for Rachel to look after their small pets for a week.

"Sold to young Johnny Foster for five dollars!" Mr. Hardy banged his hammer; Mandy, James, and Rachel sat with their mouths open in astonishment! Johnny Foster? When did he get back? And what was he up to?

Johnny Foster found Mandy, James, and Rachel as he was pushing his way through the crowd after the auction.

"We didn't know you were back," said Mandy.

"Why didn't you tell us?" asked James.

"We only got back tonight. We came straight to the auction. I didn't have time to call anybody. Where's Brandy? Is she all right?"

"She's fine," said Rachel. "So's Hero. I've been looking after them for you."

"Who's Hero?" asked Johnny, looking puzzled.

Mandy and James smiled as Rachel began to explain. She didn't miss a single detail from start to finish!

"Thanks, Rachel. It was really kind of you to look after them for me," said Johnny. "I hope your dad lets you keep Hero; you deserve him."

"But why did you bid in the auction for Rachel to look after your guinea pigs?" asked James.

"Because we're going to have to go away quite a bit in the future. My grandma's not very well and Mom will have to keep going there to look after her."

"And you'll have to go with her," Mandy said sympathetically.

"So I'll be able to look after Brandy and her babies for ages yet," said Rachel. "That's great. But I still want Dad to let me keep Hero."

"Rachel, you know I don't like animals. I'm afraid of them!"

Everyone turned at the sound of Amy Farmer's voice.

Mrs. Farmer came up behind Amy and put her hand on Amy's shoulders, smiling at Rachel as she did so.

"Well, Rachel does like animals, Amy," she said. "And there's no reason why she shouldn't look after them occasionally, is there?"

"I think your father said Rachel could look after the guinea pigs in his garage," said James. "You won't have to go near them, Amy. Your house is a long way from the garage."

Amy turned red and said nothing.

"Come on, Amy. It's not going to hurt, is it?" pleaded Rachel.

"Rachel's right," said Mrs. Farmer. "And as James said, the house *is* a long way from the garage. You don't even need to see the guinea pigs."

"And you were bitten by a *dog*, not by a guinea pig," said Rachel.

Without a glance at any of them, Amy turned and pushed her way through the crowd.

Eight

Rachel came around to Animal Ark after school the following day. She almost burst through the door in excitement. "You'll never guess what!" she said.

Mandy grinned and shook her head. She had a feeling she was going to find out very soon!

"Mom and Dad have said I can have Hero! As long as he stays in the garage I can keep him."

"Rachel, that's fantastic!" Mandy put her arm around the younger girl and gave her a hug. What great news! Everything had worked out so well: Johnny Foster had someone to care for his guinea pigs when he needed it, and Rachel had, at last, gotten a pet of her own. Things couldn't be better.

"Johnny picked up Brandy and the babies after the auction last night," Rachel continued. "And Mom and Dad found me crying in my bedroom later, although I tried not to let anybody see how upset I was."

"When are you going to get Hero?" Mandy asked.

"Dad's got to make a hutch for him first. It'll take him a few days, so I don't think I'll be able to get him until the weekend."

Mandy was thoughtful. There was an old hutch in the shed. She had kept her rabbits in it until Mom and Dad had bought her a bigger one for her birthday. It wasn't fantastic, but it would certainly do.

"I think you might be able to get Hero a little bit sooner," she said.

Rachel's eyes opened wide. "How?"

Mandy explained about the old rabbit hutch.

"Could I really have it? Really?" Rachel's eyes were sparkling now.

"Of course you can, if it's still in one piece. Let's go to the shed and have a look."

The hutch had been covered by old cloths, and when Mandy wriggled it free from under some bags of potting soil, they saw that it just needed cleaning up, and it would be perfect.

Even so, Rachel examined the hutch carefully. She opened the door and checked that the catch would close securely. She made sure that there were no holes in the chicken wire, and she studied the sleeping compartment. She turned the hutch around and around, checking the wood, and then finally tipped it up and examined the base for holes. Mandy was impressed with the care she took.

"It's fantastic, Mandy. Are you sure your mom and dad won't mind me having it?"

"I'll check with them first," said Mandy, "but I'm sure they won't."

The two girls stood up and brushed themselves off. Moving the hutch had thrown up a lot of dust!

"And we've got plenty of food, and sawdust and straw for bedding; you can have some of that to start with. And I'll see if there's an old water bottle that Simon might let you have."

"Thanks, Mandy!" Rachel was so excited that she could hardly keep still.

"Come on," said Mandy. "We'd better go and sort things out. Then we've got some work to do."

"Have a look in that drawer over there," said Simon, when Mandy asked him about the water bottle. "There's some stuff that could be cleaned, and quite a lot that needs to be thrown out. Why don't you make that one of

your jobs for tonight, Rachel? But check with Mandy
before you throw anything away."

"We'll do it together," said Mandy. "But first I need to
check with Mom that it's okay for Rachel to have the
hutch."

It was. In fact Dr. Emily was pleased that it was going
to be used again, instead of just cluttering up the shed.

The two girls went back to the shed and started to
prepare the hutch. Rachel wanted it to be absolutely
perfect for its new resident.

"I scrubbed and disinfected it before I put it away,"
said Mandy, "so it only needs a quick brushing out."

It didn't take long for them to do that, and to put
straw in the sleeping quarters and sawdust on the floor.
Then they carried the hutch to the porch, to wait for the
journey to Mr. Farmer's garage.

Back in the treatment room, they emptied out the
drawer. There were two water bottles in there, but
one had to be thrown away. The second had a plastic
cap that had been gnawed by some overenthusiastic
animal!

"It'll do until you can get a new top," said Mandy. "It
fits well enough, so it won't leak. Now, can I leave you
to finish this while I go out and see to the rabbits? I've
hardly seen them today and they need a cuddle."

Rachel grinned. She would have her very own guinea

pig to cuddle before long. "Of course, Mandy. I'll finish up here and then start cleaning out the cages if you're not back."

"Great. Then we'll call Johnny Foster to see if we can pick up Hero after we've finished here. I'll call James, too; he might want to help."

Rachel nodded and smiled. She could hardly believe that she was going to have her own pet at last. And that very evening, too!

Mandy closed the door to the shed after seeing to the rabbits and found to her surprise that it had started to snow again. Thick flakes swirled from the dark sky. She had better get the sled out again. There was yet another hutch to transport across the snow!

Rachel had finished cleaning out the drawer and had cleared the dirty bedding from those cages that needed it. She was talking to the puppy through the bars of his cage when Mandy came in.

"Poor little thing," she said. "I think he's lonely, Mandy."

"Yes, he probably is." Mandy went to the cage and put her finger through the mesh so that she could scratch the puppy's ear. He put his head to one side and closed his eyes. He obviously enjoyed it! "Never mind. He'll be back with his owner tomorrow."

"Thank goodness for that," said Rachel. "I wouldn't like my guinea pig to be all alone."

Mandy smiled. It was good to hear Rachel describe Hero as "her" guinea pig. In no time at all he would be!

"Do you want to call Johnny now? And then I'll call James."

Rachel came back and said that they could pick up Hero that evening, and it was fine with her dad, too. And James wanted to help transport Hero to his new home. He'd been involved from the beginning, and he didn't want to miss out now that there was to be a happy ending!

"By the way, have you heard the news about the auction?" James asked. "Dad bumped into Julian Hardy outside the Fox and Goose. The auction raised more than a thousand dollars for the animal sanctuary."

"A thousand dollars!" Mandy was delighted. It would keep the animal sanctuary running for some time. "I'll call Betty later and congratulate her."

It was still snowing when Mandy and Rachel stepped outside. The big flakes were fat and dry; it was going to stick again.

Rachel was almost running along the path of Animal Ark, pulling the sled behind her as if it weighed nothing. She had a lot to be pleased about.

When Mandy and Rachel arrived at Johnny Foster's

house they found a light on in the shed. James was already there with Johnny. James was holding Brandy and stroking her gently, while Johnny held Hero between his cupped hands.

"Can I come and see him sometimes?" he asked Rachel.

"Of course, come whenever you like."

"I'm going to miss him," he said. "And the others."

"Have you found homes for them?" asked Mandy.

"Two homes," said Johnny. "One of the boys in my class is taking one, Rachel's taking Hero, and I'm going to put an ad in the post office for the other two. Mom thinks I should find homes for them quite easily."

"I think she's right," said James. "They're really beautiful guinea pigs. I'd take one myself if Mom and Dad would let me."

"Me, too," said Mandy.

Rachel was getting impatient. Now that Hero was almost hers, she couldn't wait to get him into his new home. She wouldn't feel that he really belonged to her until he was safely installed in the garage.

Rachel was jumping from one foot to the other, as if she was too impatient to stand on both feet at once! She didn't want to hurry Johnny, though; he was saying goodbye to Hero and he needed to be able to do it properly.

Mandy took Brandy from James, and James bent to

pick up one of the other babies from the hutch. Mandy stroked the guinea pig's soft brown-and-white fur. She really was a beauty. Her eyes were bright and healthy and her whiskers twitched inquisitively.

"Actually," said Johnny at last, "I've been thinking about it, and I'm going to ask Mom if I can keep one of the babies. My other guinea pig died, and she might let me keep one to make up for Bramble."

Mandy knew that Bramble had been Brandy's mate and the babies' father. Johnny must have been very sad when Bramble had died; what could be better than to have one of his children to remember him by?

"That's a great idea," Mandy said. "I'm sure your mom will let you."

"Yes, I think she might," said Johnny, his face breaking into a smile.

He handed Hero over to Rachel, giving him one last stroke as he did so. "Thanks for looking after him, Rachel. He doesn't just sit in the nest moping anymore. He runs around with the rest of the babies, and he gets his fair share of the food, too."

Rachel smiled. "I think Hero's very clever," she said. "He might be small but he's got a lot of brains."

Everyone laughed and Hero nodded his head up and down, as if in agreement.

"See, I told you he was clever," said Rachel. She lifted

the little guinea pig close to her face and whispered to him. "Time to go home now, Hero."

She turned and carried him out of the shed. She lifted off the old cloths that they'd used to protect the hutch from the snow and bent down to open the door. "In you go now, boy." Carefully, Rachel placed the guinea pig into the sleeping compartment of the hutch, then closed the door securely. Mandy noticed that she was careful to make sure that the door could not open accidentally.

"Off to the Hotel Farmer," said James. "High-class accommodation for the distinguished pet."

Johnny waved to them from the doorway of the shed.

"He looks sad," said Mandy.

"He'll be all right once he knows he can keep one of the babies," said James.

"Yes, I think you're right. I just hope Mrs. Foster does let him keep one."

Rachel was ahead of them, pulling the sled quickly through the snow. She was eager to be home!

Mr. Farmer was waiting for them when they reached the garage. They saw him get up from his desk in the office; he waved and came over to them.

"My word, that's a handsome hutch. Hero's going to be very comfortable in there. Thank you very much, Mandy."

"Should we put him in the back, where he was before, Dad?" asked Rachel.

"Yes, and you can help me carry the hutch to its new home," Mr. Farmer replied.

Soon the hutch was standing on an old wooden table against the back wall of the garage.

Mandy had found an old food dish for Hero as well as the water bottle, and they were both now in the hutch with the clean sawdust and bedding.

"A guinea pig heaven," said James.

Mandy, James, and Rachel, together with Mr. Farmer, all clustered around the hutch to look at it.

"Anyone would think we were waiting for something dramatic to happen," said Mandy.

Hero, as if he had heard and understood Mandy's words, suddenly emerged from the sleeping compartment and wandered into the main area of the hutch. He came up to the chicken wire and stared at the little group. Soon he was sitting right in the middle of his food dish and enjoying a good meal.

"Just imagine if we sat in the middle of our dinner plates," said Mandy.

"A bit messy," said James. "Gravy and carrots on the seat of your jeans."

Mr. Farmer looked at his watch.

"I think I'd better get home," said Mandy. "It must be nearly bedtime."

"Well, thanks for all your help," said Mr. Farmer as he

waved good-bye to Mandy and James. "And the hutch is terrific. I won't need to make one now."

Mandy smiled. "I'm glad Hero's found a good home," she said.

Mandy and James said good-bye at the post office, and Mandy pulled the sled the short distance to Animal Ark. Snow was falling furiously and a fierce wind was blowing. It was a perfect end to a very satisfying day.

But when Mandy arrived home she found Mom and Dad waiting for her in the kitchen. And they didn't look at all pleased.

Nine

Mandy looked in dismay at her parents' faces; she felt her heart sink. What on earth was the matter? Had she done something wrong?

"I think we can be fairly sure that it wasn't you who put the puppy in Woolly's cage, Mandy," said Dr. Adam. "So it must have been Rachel."

Mandy's heart sank even farther. She remembered how sorry Rachel had been for the puppy, and worried that he might be lonely. It must have been Rachel. No one else would do such a foolish thing.

"We don't have to tell you, Mandy, about the risk of crossinfection, or the danger of Woolly harming the puppy," said Dr. Emily. "But why did Rachel do it? Can you explain?"

Mandy was close to tears. She had wanted to help Rachel by letting her come to Animal Ark, but it all seemed to have gone wrong now.

"Why do you think Rachel did it?" Dr. Emily asked again.

"She was worried about the puppy. She thought he was lonely. I told her he was going back to his owner tomorrow. She must have done it while I was on the phone with James; I left her by herself in the residential unit."

It was all too much for Mandy. Now her parents would think that she'd behaved irresponsibly, too. Tears began to trickle down her face.

Dr. Emily put her arm around Mandy's shoulder and gave her a hug. "It wasn't your fault, Mandy; we're not blaming you. But obviously this could be very serious; we're going to have to tell both of the owners in case either of the dogs becomes ill. We can't just pretend it didn't happen."

Mandy nodded through her tears. Poor Mom and Dad. They were the ones who were going to have to take the blame if anything went wrong. Mandy reached for a tissue and blew her nose.

"I'm sorry," she managed to say. "I'm really, really sorry. I'll tell Rachel not to come anymore."

"Well, let's decide about that later," said Dr. Emily. She pulled out a chair from the table for Mandy to sit on. "When Rachel comes around tomorrow, one of us will have a word with her. If she does keep on coming, she mustn't be left alone for even a minute."

Mandy nodded. If Rachel did come back to Animal Ark, she'd watch her like a hawk!

Later, Mandy went into the residential unit to have a look at the two dogs. Both of them were sleeping peacefully, unaware of all the fuss. With a bit of luck, they'd both be perfectly all right.

In bed that night, Mandy thought of what Betty Hilder had said about needing to know what you were doing when you were looking after animals. Most people wanted to be kind, but ignorance could sometimes have terrible consequences. If Rusty the fox had been tamed, he wouldn't be able to cope in the wild. Rachel thought she was doing the right thing because the puppy was lonely, but she hadn't realized what sorts of things could happen.

Mandy didn't want to think about it anymore. She'd have to try to sort things out in the morning.

The next morning, Mandy woke to find the roads and the stone walls had disappeared beneath a fresh blanket of snow.

"No school again today," said Dr. Adam when Mandy came downstairs. "The snowplows are out, but it will probably be lunchtime before the roads are clear again."

"How are the dogs?" Mandy asked nervously.

"They seem absolutely fine. They can go home today as planned. I'll ask the owners to keep a special eye on them. But I don't really think there'll be any problems." Dr. Emily smiled. "Cheer up, Mandy. It could have been worse."

Mom's confidence made Mandy feel a little better.

"What are we going to do about Rachel?" asked Mandy.

"Why don't you give her a call and see if she wants to come up here this morning? Tell her we need to talk about what happened."

Mandy hesitated. She wasn't eager to confront Rachel with last night's episode; she knew Rachel was so happy at the moment, now that she had Hero. Still, Mandy knew that it was her responsibility to tell her.

"I'll give her a call now," she said.

"Good girl." Mom finished her tea and headed for the clinic. Snow or no snow, there was always work to be done at Animal Ark.

Mandy picked up the phone reluctantly. She wasn't looking forward to making this call.

"Hi, Mandy!" came Rachel's excited voice. Mandy's heart sank. She didn't want to spoil Rachel's good mood.

"Isn't it fantastic! All this snow and no school! You'll never guess what I did. I've moved Hero into a car trunk!"

"You've done what?" Mandy's surprise drove all other thoughts from her mind.

"Don't worry; I'll leave the trunk open so Hero's not in the dark. You see, I got some books out of the library about guinea pigs and I was reading one of them last night. It said it wasn't a good idea to keep them in a garage because of car exhaust fumes."

"I think that means an ordinary small garage, not a big workshop like your dad's."

"Oh," said Rachel.

"Anyway, where is this car trunk?"

"In an old garage around the back of the main garage. It's an old car and it's been there for ages. It's got a lovely big trunk with carpet in it. It's really quite cozy."

"Well, if you think Hero will be all right there . . ." said Mandy.

"He will. He'll be fine."

Mandy took a deep breath. "Rachel, there's something I want to talk to you about."

She told Rachel everything that had happened, and that her parents wanted to talk to her.

"But he was so lonely, Mandy. I thought it was the best thing to do."

"I suppose you did. But it wasn't very sensible, Rachel."

"I'm sorry. I didn't think it might be dangerous. Are the dogs all right?" There was a note of anxiety in Rachel's voice now.

"Yes, they seem to be fine. I don't think you need to worry about them."

Mandy breathed a sigh of relief when she put the phone down. Thank goodness that was over and done with!

But when Rachel arrived things weren't as bad as Mandy had feared. Dr. Emily had a quiet word with Rachel about the responsibilities of working with animals, and how she must never do anything without checking with someone first, even if she thought she was doing the right thing.

Rachel accepted what Dr. Emily had to say very bravely. But she was upset about what she'd done, now that she understood why she shouldn't have done it.

"I just didn't think, Dr. Emily. I wanted the puppy to be happy. I'm very sorry I did the wrong thing."

Dr. Emily looked serious but her voice was kind. "I can see that you really are sorry, Rachel. I hope you understand now why we have to be so strict about such things."

She went on to explain that Rachel could continue to help out at Animal Ark as long as she never did anything again without asking.

"Perhaps it would be better if I just concentrated on looking after Hero," Rachel said. "I've really enjoyed coming here, but now I've got Hero. I need to spend time with him."

"I think that's a very sensible decision," Dr. Emily said.

Mandy agreed. Rachel had really been a bit of a handful!

"Can I just stay for this morning, though?"

"Of course you can," said Dr. Emily. "And I think you and Mandy had better go and say good-bye to your old friends. Their owners are coming to pick them up shortly."

Woolly's ears were pricked up sharply; she looked intently out through the cage door, tail wagging. "You know, I'm sure she knows she's going home," said Mandy. "Sometimes dogs seem to have some sort of sixth sense."

She had hardly finished speaking when Simon appeared. "Come on, Woolly, old girl, home time." He lifted Woolly's leash off the hook by the cage. The dog stood up, tail wagging even harder. She definitely knew where she was going!

"See what I mean?" said Mandy. "Do you think she could have smelled her owner through two doors and across a couple of rooms, Simon?"

"I wouldn't be surprised," said Simon. "Some dogs are incredible."

Woolly licked Simon's hands, as if to say, "And I'm one of them!"

"Would you like to have one last cuddle with the lonely puppy?" Simon asked Rachel, teasing her. "His owner's in the waiting room, too."

"Yes, please," said Rachel. She turned red. Everybody seemed to know how silly she'd been!

Mandy opened the cage door and took the little puppy out. He opened one eye lazily as he heard the door open. He obviously had no idea that his owner was in the waiting room; he was too busy snoozing.

"Come on, sleepyhead," said Mandy. The tired little dog nuzzled up under Mandy's chin and promptly went to sleep again.

Simon delivered Woolly to her owner, then came back for the puppy. Mandy and Rachel gave the little dog a final pat, but he didn't even open an eye when Simon took him from Mandy's arms.

"You must get really sad when they go home," said Rachel. "I'm going to miss that little puppy."

"You do sometimes," said Mandy. "You get really fond of some of the animals. But then there are always new ones to take their place. And it's much better for the animals to be at home with their owners."

Rachel smiled, thinking about Hero waiting at home for her. "I expect you're right."

The two girls had just started on the chores when a telephone call came for Mandy. It was James.

"Coming sledding?"

"Rachel's here. Do you mind if she comes along, too?"

"No, of course not. She can pick up her sled on the way over here. Then we'll go up to High Cross."

"Great. How's Blackie getting on?"

"Oh, he's nearly better now, thanks. But if he notices anyone looking at him he starts to limp for sympathy."

Mandy laughed. "See you soon, James."

Half an hour later, Mandy and Rachel were dressed for blizzard conditions. But when they stepped outside, they found it had stopped snowing and the wind had dropped. The heavy blanket of snow muffled ordinary everyday noises; the whole world was white and silent.

"It's beautiful," Rachel said.

Mandy nodded. It certainly was.

By the time they got to the garage, they were already

feeling tired. Wading through the deep snow had made their legs ache.

"Let's have five minutes' rest," said Rachel. "Then you can come and see Hero."

"Johnny Foster called," shouted Mr. Farmer as they stepped into the garage. "He wanted you to know that his mother's letting him keep one of the baby guinea pigs."

Mandy and Rachel smiled at each other. "Isn't that great news?" said Rachel. "I know just how he must be feeling."

Mandy followed the younger girl across the garage to a door at the back. Apart from Mr. Farmer's shouted message, it was unusually quiet in there. Two of the mechanics were drinking tea and reading their newspapers. The snow had slowed down business for the garage, too.

"The car's in this old garage," called Rachel when they were outside. "I think Hero really likes it in here." She went through the door and held it open for Mandy to follow.

"I can't see it," said Mandy, puzzled. She was looking into a completely empty space.

Rachel turned to her with a stunned face.

"Neither can I," she said. "The car is gone."

Ten

"Dad! Dad!" Rachel rushed back into the garage and across to the office where Mr. Farmer was having a quiet mug of coffee.

"Where's the old car, Dad? Someone's taken it. Where is it?" Rachel pulled at her father's sleeve so hard that he almost spilled his coffee.

"Hang on a minute, Rachel. What's the matter? What car?"

"The one in the outside garage. The old blue Ford. I put Hero in there because of the fumes."

"What fumes?" Mr. Farmer looked totally bewildered. "Rachel, calm down and tell me exactly what's wrong."

He put his mug down and placed his arm around his daughter's shoulder. "Come on. Tell me what's wrong."

But Rachel was far too upset to explain anything clearly. Mandy did it for her, telling Mr. Farmer what had happened. She saw his face grow tense with worry.

"Well, I'm afraid this is serious, Rachel," said Mr. Farmer. "The car's been taken to the junkyard. One of the men has been wanting to take it for ages; and he chose today of all days. He's crazy if you ask me, through all this snow."

"But what about Hero? What's going to happen to him?"

Rachel was in floods of tears and Mandy's heart began to beat hard with fear. Mandy had seen the junkyard in Walton. She pictured the old cars, crushed flat by giant machinery. Nothing inside one of those cars could possibly survive.

"We've got to get to the junkyard, Mr. Farmer, before it's too late." But even as she spoke, Mandy realized how difficult it was going to be. Her parents had said that the roads wouldn't be clear until after lunch; anything could happen by then!

"Perhaps they won't have gotten to the junkyard yet; not with all the snow around and the roads blocked," Rachel said hopefully.

Mr. Farmer shook his head. "I'm afraid they will,

Rachel. The road to Walton's clear now. In any case, the man's got a big four-wheel drive pickup truck; he'll get through this with no trouble."

"What's the matter? Who's in trouble?"

"James! What are you doing here?" Mandy could have hugged him. James was always so levelheaded, it was good to have him around in a crisis.

James had rushed headlong into the garage about a foot behind Blackie. It was obviously a case of Blackie taking James for a walk, rather than the other way around!

"I got fed up waiting for you two, so I thought I'd meet you down here and give Blackie a short walk at the same time. He's a lot better now. You'd hardly know he'd been injured. He won't be coming sledding, of course."

Mandy gave Blackie a hug. She felt she needed it just as much as Blackie did. She told James about Hero.

"We really need a four-wheel-drive vehicle to get there," said Mr. Farmer. "Even though the main road's clear now; it could be tricky on the side roads. As you can see, my old Jeep's in twenty pieces at the moment."

He pointed to a Jeep in one of the far corners of the garage. The two wheels that Mandy could see were both off. It definitely wasn't going to be of much use.

"What about your father's Land Rover, Mandy?" asked James. "Do you think he'd be able to drive us?"

Mandy looked doubtful. Dr. Adam would need the Land Rover if he was called out for an emergency.

"Oh, please say yes, Mandy. Please try." Rachel's words came out in a shudder of sobs. Then Mandy thought of Hero and the horrible thing that might happen to him. She had to try!

"Use the phone in the office," said Mr. Farmer, as if reading Mandy's mind.

Mandy raced across the garage. There was no time to lose.

"Well, office hours are finished," Dr. Adam said thoughtfully. "It's been very quiet this morning, what with the snow. I've got one routine call to make and then I suppose we could give it a try. I'll be with you as soon as I can. But mind you, if any calls come through, they'll have to take priority. We're not an animal rescue center, you know."

"Thanks, Dad!" Mandy put the phone down. She felt much more optimistic now that she knew her father was on his way.

"What if there's an emergency?" asked James.

"There's a phone in the Land Rover," said Mandy. "Dad's already said that if there's a call, it will have to take priority."

Mr. Farmer nodded. "Of course it will. Now, why don't you three go and wait outside until Dr. Adam arrives."

Once outside they hardly spoke. They were all too worried about Hero to say anything. Mandy kept looking at her watch. Although it was only twenty-five minutes before she saw the Land Rover come into sight, it seemed much longer.

"This is your friendly neighborhood rescue mission," Dr. Adam said with a grin. "It's a good thing there's all this snow, Rachel, otherwise we might have been too busy to help out. I've left Dr. Emily setting a broken leg, but apart from that there's not much happening."

Rachel sat beside Mandy, clutching her hands together, her face white. She didn't say a word. Every now and then she lifted her head to look out the window, as if she expected to see Hero there.

The Land Rover traveled the plowed and sanded road to Walton with ease. Even so, Mandy thought the journey would never end.

Blackie was in the back, safely installed behind the dog guard, and Mandy thought about his last journey there, just a few days ago, when he was in so much pain. She was glad there was nothing seriously wrong with him.

By the time they turned in at the gates of the junkyard, Mandy's heart felt as if it was beating at twice its normal rate. Would Hero be here? Would he be all right?

Everyone jumped out of the Land Rover the instant Dr. Adam cut the ignition. In front of them, and reaching as high as a house, was a mountain of crushed metal.

Dr. Adam headed for the office while Mandy, James, and Rachel ran around the yard, looking anxiously for a small wooden hutch. There were piles of rusting cars, heaps of old tires; the yard overflowed with discarded car scraps. There was no sign of a hutch.

"I can't see it anywhere!" Rachel was beginning to cry again. Mandy felt that she was about to join her when Dr. Adam came striding across the yard, looking very serious indeed.

"It's not here. There's been no blue Ford delivered today."

"Well, where can it be?" asked James. "It has to be here."

"No, it doesn't," said Dr. Adam. "The man in the office said there's another junkyard that just opened. Unfortunately, it's on the other side of Walton."

"We'll never find him," said Rachel. "Never. It's going to be too late." Her voice sounded scratched and small.

"We'll do our very best," said Dr. Adam. "Don't give

up, Rachel. Sit beside me and help me find the way to the new junkyard."

Rachel sat next to Dr. Adam in the Land Rover, reading out the directions the man in the office had written down for them. Mandy could see that it helped Rachel to have something to do.

"Oh, no!"

Mandy looked up at the sound of her father's voice.

"Construction," said Dr. Adam. "The traffic is being diverted the long way around town. This could take hours!"

Mandy gripped the back of the seat tightly. Would they ever get there?

The traffic inched slowly forward, then came to a halt. There were traffic lights up ahead and a long line of cars in front of the Land Rover.

James sighed. Dr. Adam tapped his fingers on the steering wheel as he quickly read through the directions once more. Rachel held her hands to her face, as if she couldn't bear to look at the long line of traffic. Even Blackie shifted uneasily in the back.

"Got it!" Dr. Adam said. Just as he spoke the lights changed to green, and the cars began to move again. "I think I know a shortcut."

Dr. Adam turned left down the next road and then drove through a maze of back streets. Mandy was completely lost. But at last they came out on the main road on the other side of Walton. And within a few minutes, they spotted the new junkyard coming up on their left. In no time at all, they were in the new office.

"We had an old blue Ford come in early this morning. But I don't know what's happened to it. We'd better take a look around." The man pulled on his coat and they followed him out of the door.

It didn't look much different from the other junkyard; piles of old and rusting cars were everywhere. They followed the man around, walking quickly.

Suddenly, Rachel gave a small scream. "It's the car! Look!"

Mandy felt dizzy with fear as she followed Rachel's pointing finger with her eyes. There, high in the air, was a blue car, swinging from an enormous crane. The car was held in the clutches of a huge metal claw. Mandy knew exactly what would happen next. She had seen it before. The claw would release its grip and the car would fall onto the mountain of rusting metal. And Hero would fall with it. It would kill him. There was no doubt about it.

For a time, everyone seemed paralyzed. They watched as the metal claw swung slowly around toward a pile of old cars. Any second now, those giant claws would open and it would all be too late.

"Quick! We've got to do something!"

Almost without thinking, Mandy rushed down the yard until she was standing in front of the crane. She jumped up and down, waving her arms in the air and shouting "Stop! Stop!"

Within seconds she was followed by the others. They, too, waved their arms and shouted. The car was right over the middle of the pile of metal now. At any moment, it would be dropped onto it. The crane driver had to notice them. He had to!

And to their relief, he did. The man stopped the crane and climbed down from the driver's compartment.

Rachel almost fainted with relief. She leaned against Dr. Adam and he put his arm around her. Tears streamed down her face.

The crane driver was coming toward them. He didn't look too pleased.

Dr. Adam explained what had happened and the driver's face softened. "The animal's not here," he said.

The three friends groaned. Just when they thought they'd found him. Where on earth could Hero be?

"We always check the cars over before they go to be crushed," the man explained. "And we strip them down of any parts that we can use. Of course, we always open the trunk; might be a useful tire in there. But you don't expect to find a guinea pig in a hutch!"

"Well, where is he?" asked Dr. Adam.

"One of our men lives over near Welford. He took it to the animal sanctuary. It was the only thing we could think of; it's closer than the ASPCA."

The animal sanctuary! Mandy almost laughed out loud with relief. One thing was for sure, Hero would be safe with Betty Hilder!

"Looks like we need to go back to Welford," said James.

"Can we use your phone to check that he's arrived?" asked Dr. Adam.

The man nodded.

The group of friends clustered eagerly around Dr. Adam as he dialed the animal sanctuary. It was taking Betty a long time to answer. Mandy felt her relief change to anxiety once more. What would the man have done with Hero if he'd arrived at the animal sanctuary to find no one there?

Dr. Adam put the phone down. "No answer, I'm afraid."

Just when it seemed as though Hero was safe! The friends walked slowly back to the Land Rover.

They were almost back in Welford when the car phone rang. Mandy heard her father's brisk, professional voice promising to be somewhere almost immediately.

"There's a litter of sick pups out toward High Cross. I'm afraid I'm going to have to drop you in the village and you'll have to make your own way to the animal sanctuary from there."

Mandy nodded. You couldn't ignore a litter of sick puppies; her father certainly wouldn't. But it was yet another delay. And they still couldn't be sure that Hero had been safely delivered to the animal sanctuary.

Dr. Adam dropped them off outside the garage, and they collected Rachel's sled from there. Mandy felt as though she had spent a lot of time lately transporting guinea pigs through the snow!

"We'll have to get the bus," said James. "There's one coming now. We'll catch it if we hurry."

They ran toward the bus stop. They got there just in time. Blackie seemed especially happy — he loved riding in buses!

"I hope Hero's here," said Rachel as they jumped from the bus at the sanctuary stop. Mandy and James both hoped he was, too!

Mandy raced down the path ahead of the others. Betty answered the door immediately.

"I've been expecting you," she said. "Your father called just after he dropped you off, to say that you were coming. I'd just gotten back from shopping; that's why I wasn't in when your father first called."

"Is Hero here?" Rachel almost pushed Mandy out of the way.

Betty smiled. "Why don't you come and see for yourself, Rachel?"

Hero *was* there. And he looked none the worse for his adventure. He sat calmly in the middle of his food bowl, helping himself to a nice fat sunflower seed. He looked as though he hadn't a care in the world.

"He's wondering what all the fuss was about," said James as Hero poked his nose through the chicken wire of the hutch. He certainly did seem to have a puzzled expression on his face.

"Oh, Hero! I'm never going to let you out of my sight again," said Rachel. She opened the door of the hutch and held the guinea pig gently in the palm of her hand. She stroked him with one finger, then tucked him under her chin. "He likes it there," she said.

"So, you're never going to let him out of your sight again," said James.

"Never!" Rachel said firmly.

"That should be interesting," said James. "Can you imagine it, Mandy? Guinea pig in the bathroom. Guinea pig in the kitchen. Guinea pig at school."

They all laughed. "You know what I mean, James," said Rachel.

They waved good-bye to Betty and set off back down

to the village, with Rachel pulling Hero on the sled. She wouldn't let anyone else help her. Blackie was very interested in the contents of the hutch, but James kept him firmly on his leash.

"I think Blackie would be more of a problem for Hero than even an iron claw," said Mandy.

"You know what? I'm going to give a month's pocket money to the animal sanctuary as a thank-you," Rachel said a little while later.

"I think that's a wonderful idea," said Mandy.

James agreed. They plodded on through the deep

snow, and before long they were back in Welford. They all had lunch at Rachel's house.

"It's very nice of you," said Mandy, when Mrs. Farmer invited them to stay.

"Well, I think the least I can do is offer you both lunch, after all the kindness you've shown to Rachel."

"And Hero," Rachel added.

"Amy and I have been having a little talk," said Mrs. Farmer. "And we both think that Hero would be much safer in Rachel's room."

Rachel was absolutely thrilled. "Can I really keep him in my room? You really don't mind, Amy?"

"Well, I don't think I'll be going in your room very often," Amy said.

"But I know that Amy doesn't want to be frightened of animals forever," said Mrs. Farmer.

"Just because of one bad-tempered dog," said Amy.

"So we'll take it slowly and gently with Hero; let Amy get to know him in her own good time."

"I'll help you," said Rachel. "Really I will, Amy."

"Thanks, Rachel. I'm glad you won't be at the garage all the time now. It's boring without you."

Mandy and James smiled at each other. It looked as though Amy really was making an effort to get over her fear of animals.

"Are you two coming sledding this afternoon?" Mandy asked.

"I don't think so," Rachel said. "I want to put Hero in my room and just play with him for a while."

"You just don't want to let him out of your sight, do you?" James said teasingly.

Rachel laughed. "Amy might want to go," she suggested.

But Amy shook her head. "I think I'll stay with Rachel," she said. "We can go sledding tomorrow."

Mandy and James said good-bye at the Farmers' back door.

"Thanks for everything, Mandy. And you, James. I don't think I'll ever be able to thank you enough."

"You don't have to," said Mandy. "But Rachel, just promise me one thing, will you?"

"What's that?"

"If ever you feel one of your bright ideas coming on, just talk to me first, please."

Rachel smiled. "I will," she said.

Mandy and James waved from the gate. They were looking forward to their afternoon's sledding. Mandy thought they deserved it!